Arthur Herzog

HEAT

SIMON AND SCHUSTER · NEW YORK

Published by Simon and Schuster
A Division of Gulf & Western Corporation
Simon & Schuster Building
Rockefeller Center
1230 Avenue of the Americas
New York, New York 10020

Designed by Eve Metz
Manufactured in the United States of America

1 2 3 4 5 6 7 8 9 10

Library of Congress Cataloging in Publication Data
Herzog, Arthur.
Heat.
I. Title.
PZ4.H58He   [PS3558.E796]   813'.5'4   77–469
ISBN 0-671-22532-4

ACKNOWLEDGMENTS

The author wishes to thank the following organizations and individuals for their invaluable advice and technical help:

National Oceanic and Atmospheric Administration: Dr. J. Murray Mitchell, Ed Weigel. NOAA Geophysical Dynamics Laboratory, Princeton, New Jersey: Harold Frazer. NOAA Environmental Research Laboratory, Boulder, Colorado: Carl A. Posey, Sam O. Honess.

Institute for Environmental Studies, University of Wisconsin: John Ross, Drs. Alden McClellan, E. W. Wahl.

National Academy of Sciences: Drs. Charles E. Fritz, John Perry.

Center for the Study of Short-Lived Phenomenon, Smithsonian Institution: Charles Citron, Shirley Maina, David Squire, James C. Cornel. I might note that the Center, with reports on natural events, partially inspired CRISES.

National Center for Atmospheric Research: Dr. Stephen Schneider.

Dr. Jerry Grey, Brad Byers, Mac Megaha, Charles Crum, Dr. Gregory Herzog, Naomi Rubenstein, William E. Bernard, Jr., Judy Feiffer, Dr. Michael Baden, Diana Grant.

Special thanks to Drs. Mitchell and Grey and to Ross Wetzsteon and Don McKinney for reading the manuscript.

And to my invaluable editors who worked on this—Phyllis Grann and Joni Evans.

FOR MY BROTHERS AND SISTERS IN SPIRIT

We have seen that when a people in peril can save themselves only at the cost of a quick and dramatic change in their habits and beliefs, they usually prefer to perish.

—L. Sprague and Catherine de Camp,
Citadels of Mystery

. . . if man is not yet in nature's league as a potent climate-regulating force, he is almost certainly destined to become such a force in the rather near future. Of special concern in this connection is the dangerous circumstance that man may well arrive at that point *inadvertently* before he arrives there deliberately, and that he will find himself unequipped to arrest or reverse undesirable climatic developments that he may have set in motion unwittingly. From any point of view, therefore, it is a matter of some urgency that we identify the causes of modern-day climatic instability, and make an accurate determination of man's impact on world climate both present and future.*

Present emission of energy is about 1/15,000 of the absorbed solar flux. But if the present rate of growth continued for 250 years emissions would reach 100% of the absorbed solar flux. The resulting increase in the earth's temperature would be about 50 C.—a condition totally unsuited for human habitation.†

* J. Murray Mitchell, "A Reassessment of Atmospheric Pollution as a Cause of Long-term Changes of Global Temperature."
† Robert U. Ayres and Allen V. Kneese, *Economic and Ecological Effects of a Stationary State*, Resources for the Future, Reprint 99, December 1972, p. 16. Quoted in Robert L. Heilbroner, *The Human Prospect*, p. 51.

Mɪsᴛʏ ᴅᴀᴡɴ. Gray ocean. A colorless cloud covered a distant mountaintop like a ragged hat.

Tito rested at the tiller while José, Carlos and João brooded by the lines. Normally six men worked the stubby craft, but the two cousins had jobs in Funchal that day and didn't want to come. The brothers had gone to sea anyway because four could handle the *traineira* when the water was calm and the catches small.

The cousins were right not to sail, Tito thought bitterly. He himself did not enjoy working as a laborer, but at least the cousins would be paid. He glared at the flat gray sea. At one time, a line with one hundred hooks brought up fifteen espada or more and you needed a crew of six to pull them up. The ocean, generous then, was selfish now. The brothers had drifted since midnight, dropping the weighted lines, retrieving, rebaiting the hooks with squid, dropping the lines once more, and all the ocean had yielded was a meager pile of black fish, hardly enough for the brothers Pestana to feed their families.

This was their last attempt before they went back to port. The espada swam more than a half mile down, and the fishermen had the lines out to the last foot, deeper than they had tried during the night, deeper than was usually needed. But Tito felt desperate. There had to be many espada taking the bait even then. The ocean could not continue to be so cruel . . .

The Portuguese seized an espada almost angrily. Named for the sword, it looked more like a club when held by the tail. To Tito, the fish had always seemed like an accident of God. It had the large head, wide mouth and brutally sharp teeth of a barracuda. The body was almost that of an eel, three feet long or more, three inches high, and only a half-inch thick. The peculiar shape, he believed, was due to the ocean pressure under which the animal lived.

Still, though ugly, the black creatures made good eating and the islanders prized them. Tito could have sold catches many times as large as the one before him. But even in good years espada weren't really plentiful. If they had been, Madeira could have exported them like its sweet wines. But, as far as Tito knew, the espada swam in the deep Madeiran waters only, and the outside world was hardly aware of its existence.

The sun would be up in a minute and it was time to return. Pulling together, the men raised the lines, one by one, coiling rope as they lifted. A few more espada landed on the pile but the harvest stayed scanty. Only the end of the last line remained when João spotted the brightness in the pallid water.

He pointed, gasping. A few more pulls and it thrashed on the deck. Certainly the odd fish was an espada, but different from any they had encountered. Instead of being coal black, the fish was bright red. Its jaws opened wide, as if in surprise.

"What has God done?" Tito asked in a low voice.

"The fish must be diseased," José said.

"Disease? What disease? I have heard of none."

"I do not know. A fungus perhaps?"

12

"There is no sign."

"Could the fish have been attacked by another?" Carlos questioned.

"That is silly. There are no wounds, no marks of teeth. Even if there were, why would it turn the color of cooked lobster?"

"Some strange condition of the seawater?" João suggested cautiously.

Tito shrugged. He stared with fascination at the apparition. It had almost stopped moving. "It is a very horrible fish when bright red. I do not like it."

"It is a fish created by the devil," Carlos muttered. He tried to smile at his brothers, who stood in a group at the boat's side.

"What shall we do with it? Shall we bring it back to Funchal?" José cried.

"I do not think so. Who would buy espada any more, believing them tainted? Better that we not even speak of it, or no market will be found for the other fish. Let us not bring it. Let us return it to the ocean." He sighed.

None of the brothers Pestana wanted to touch the frightening fish, so they cut the line, which had only a few more hooks in any case. Tito started the outboard and they moved away, leaving the fish to toss in the wake. In their haste, they failed to notice that two other red espada, caught on the line, had bobbed to the surface.

PART I
PRECURSORS

1
CHAPTER

RISING, LAWRENCE PICK followed an invariable routine. Having glanced regretfully at his empty bed, he exercised furiously before a tall mirror, not out of admiration for his muscular frame but to keep his movements clean and precise. For company he had the TV news, though he watched only when something interested him. His head turned as the weatherman came on.

Brought up on a farm in northeastern Pennsylvania, Lawrence Pick still looked at the weather not as something that decided if you did or didn't take an umbrella but as an all-important part of life, determining when planting or harvesting was done, or if you worked outside or inside that day. Without thinking much about it, he followed the weather closely.

". . . freakish weather prevails throughout the country as it has for the last few weeks, with drought in the far West, a heat wave in the South, exceptionally heavy snows in the Midwest, hail and high winds in the Northeast and in the mid-Atlantic states more rain. It's another nasty day in Washington, I'm afraid, with temperatures in the low forties and the rain that began falling earlier predicted to last until evening. Joggers, forget it again. But there's hope for tomorrow, folks. Would you believe it? The National Weather Service predicts sunshine! Well, it had to get better because it couldn't get worse. John?"

"You said it. Turning to sports . . ."

Having finished his exercises, Pick turned off the TV and stood a moment before the bedroom window, cursing the elements. After calisthenics he liked to jog a few miles, but the weatherman was correct—he'd been rained out again. Well, he was late, having overslept because he'd worked into the night.

Work, work, too much work, the windshield wipers seemed to be saying as he drove out of Chevy Chase for downtown Washington, D.C. Well, nobody forced him; it was his own fault that he took on so much and had trouble delegating authority. True, the position was sensitive and mistakes could be costly, but still, he let the work ethic govern his existence. Recently, even his boss had lectured him on overzealousness. Rufus Edmunston blamed Pick's social life, or lack of one. The Director had remarked in the easy, garrulous manner he affected, "I don't deny you're good at your job, Larry, but you fret too much. You'll lose perspective sooner or later. You don't have enough fun. We all need distractions, especially us in the front lines. You don't even have a steady girlfriend, right? At your age! You're by yourself too much and it makes you gloomy. There are zillions of nice girls in Washington and a handsome guy like you could have his choice. Why don't you find a gal to live with, Larry? You could even marry again. It's not against the law, you know."

"Maybe it should be," Pick replied with a grin that faded just as it began.

Edmunston laughed and replied, "Yes, maybe so."

Pick watched the wipers sweep steadily. The old man would

18

probably accuse him of worrying when he opened the sealed envelope Pick had left with his secretary the evening before. The envelope had been marked "Secret and Urgent," and the secretary had locked it in the safe for the night. It concerned a recent Siberian earthquake that the Russians had failed to report. Pick could have delayed a few days to see what happened before alerting his boss, but that might give the Sovs, as he called them, time to destroy evidence in the event (unlikely, he admitted) that the earthquake had been induced by a nuclear bomb. Besides, it wasn't in the Deputy's character to procrastinate.

Therein lay an important difference between Edmunston and himself, Pick mused. Often, the Director failed to move on things. Edmunston had what amounted to a conviction that all problems could be solved with patience, and even solve themselves mysteriously in ways that nobody predicted. The Director was against rushes to judgment, crash programs, frenetic activity in general. Pick had to agree that it could be better to do nothing than something, when you didn't understand what the something might lead to, but just the same there were instances when Edmunston's cautionary stance was a disguise for a lack of knowledge, or an exercise in the self-proclaimed optimism which the Director wore almost like a cloak to protect himself against old age.

For Pick, Edmunston sometimes failed to grasp the importance of events because he had lost touch with the latest in science. At sixty-three, the former physicist hadn't been on the "bench," as scientists call laboratory research, in more than two decades. He had moved from one major executive job to the next until, as Director of CRISES, he occupied one of the most sensitive and prestigious scientific-establishment posts in the country. Still, Pick judged his own scientific expertise to be superior. He occasionally feared that the day might come when Edmunston would fail to recognize an urgent situation for what it was, and would advise waiting at a time when delay could be fatal.

Lawrence Pick believed himself to be on the front edge of his field. A graduate of the University of Pennsylvania, he was an engineer, but only in the broadest sense. He had a double master's in engineering and environmental science from Harvard, and a Ph.D. in engineering from MIT, where he had become a full professor before the age of thirty. He had joined NASA as a senior satellite specialist, and then the Department of Defense's Advanced Research Projects Agency (ARPA), a connection which, as few except the Director knew, he still maintained. Ecology, space travel, energy technology, computers, advanced engineering—he was versed in all. For his papers, patents and concepts, especially as related to space, he had earned, he knew, the respect of his peers.

But what good was all that if he wasn't happy? All work and no play makes . . . Edmunston was right, the engineer needed a woman to lighten his life. He was only human. Pick was forty—too old to live alone. Maybe a steady girlfriend would be good for him, even a wife. But the mere thought of marriage evoked bittersweet memories of long legs and clinking bracelets. Several years ago she had departed his bed and board because he failed to make time for her. The next wife, Pick dreamed, would be different. Simple tastes, pleasant ways, sweet disposition . . . loving, gentle, tolerant of his foibles . . . she'd wave goodbye in the mornings. . . . But why should *she* put up with him either? he asked himself and became suddenly dispirited, which he blamed on the gloomy skies.

CRISES (Crisis Research Investigation and Systems Evaluation Service) had been established when even politicians con-

20

cluded that an organization specializing in disaster, present or future, was increasingly necessary because catastrophes seemed to have become a permanent part of life. The job of the multidisciplinary body was to identify, study and warn of potential environmental hazards, be they natural calamities like hurricanes and earthquakes, or unidentified diseases, or those phenomena at least partly attributable to man, like atmospheric inversions. The group was also meant to calculate the costs of avoiding disasters and of recovering from them. CRISES, in short, was to provide what Rufus Edmunston liked to call "a total global trouble picture."

Pick entered the gray Georgian building and glanced automatically at the innocent displays. A sign explained that CRISES was a respected body and a member of such groups as the International Council of Scientific Unions (ICSU). A papier-mâché globe showed the orbits of communications and weather satellites. On a large wall map, current international problems were identified by printed cards coded by color—blue for astrophysical, green for biological, brown for ecological, red for economopolitical. A rear-end projector, running continuously, presented a 2,000-year chronicle of natural disasters such as:

A.D. 526	Earthquake	Antioch, Syria	Quake killed 250,000
740–44	Epidemic	Constantinople	Bubonic plague, 200,000 died.
747–51	Black plague	Europe	75,000,000 died.
1556	Earthquake	Shensi Province, China	Quake killed more than 1,000,000, probably the largest number of fatalities from one earthquake in recorded history.

1711	Epidemic	Germany and Austria	Bubonic plague. More than 500,000 casualties.
1792	Epidemic	Egypt	Bubonic plague. 800,000 victims.
1812–13	Famine	Korea	2,500,000 perished.
1826–37	Epidemic	Continental Europe	Cholera pandemic killed millions; 900,000-plus Europeans died in 1831 alone.
1846–51	Potato famine	Ireland	1 million dead.
1881	Typhoon	China and Indochina	Oct. 8; violent storm plus tidal wave killed 300,000.
1918	War-related flu epidemic	Worldwide	21,640,000 dead.
1970	Cyclone	Bangladesh	200,000 victims plus starvation afterwards.
1978	Earthquake	Tokyo	250,000 dead.

Yellow paper drooled from a teletype machine. Pick walked over to look at the bulletins which had gone out that morning.

EVENT 710–79—ECOLOGICAL—CORPUS CHRISTI HARBOR OIL SPILL.
At 1230 GMT 9 Nov. the U.S. Coast Guard reported a major oil spill in the 4.83 kilometer harbor area at Corpus Christi, Texas. A total of 5,000,000 liters of Arabian crude oil with a high sulphur content is thought to be in the harbor.
The oil's source is unknown, but it is thought to have been a vessel. There is little or no wildlife present in this highly industrial area.

22

EVENT 711–79—BIOLOGICAL—MALARIA OUTBREAK IN INDIA.
India Public Health Services reports a severe outbreak of malaria in the northern states. The numbers of those presently afflicted with the disease may exceed 1,000,000.

EVENT 712–79—GEOPHYSICAL—HEAVY WINDS BATTER VOLCANO ISLANDS.

EVENT 713–79—GEOPHYSICAL—ICELANDIC ARCTIC PACK-ICE.
During the last two weeks the dense tongue of Arctic pack-ice that extends south to the coast of northwest Iceland near Cape Horn and makes sailing difficult or impossible has suddenly retreated. Such a retreat in fall months is rare.

A plaque presented CRISES' motto: "The Future Is Our Responsibility."

The tourists and schoolchildren who came to look at the lobby displays never seemed to notice how strongly the elevators were guarded by alert-looking men in the inconspicuous gray uniforms of CRISES' security force, or to wonder why. The hook-nosed man seated at a desk ranked as a captain. Pick had never liked him. His name was Nash and he had a cliché for everything. "Morning, Dr. Pick," Nash said heartily. He spoke with a southwestern twang. "Wet enough for you?"

"I'm renting an ark from Hertz," Pick returned.

Upstairs, his buxom but attractive secretary, Gwen, repeated, "Wet enough for you?"

"Can't anybody think of anything new to ask about the rain?" Pick complained.

Gwen followed him into his small, plainly furnished office with the morning paper and the mail, placing them on his desk. She said in a confidential tone, "You had a call at nine sharp this morning from a man named Blake at the National

Weather Service. He said it was important, but wouldn't say why. He sounded young and excitable to me."

"Later," Pick said in a distracted voice.

"Coffee?" she asked, solicitous as always.

He glanced at the clock, which said 9:25. He wanted coffee but knew that before he could drink it the phone would ring. "Thanks, no."

He skimmed the Friday morning paper standing up. The news would please the hearts of progress-loving, recession-fearing Americans. Jobs at 100 million . . . national output tops 2 trillion . . . stock averages at an all-time high . . . Project Independence was in full swing with power plants of every type opening all over (a photo of one showed fire breathing into the night). Pick frowned. Prosperity was fine, but at what price?

Stop it, he told himself. The phone rang. "Pick," he answered.

"Larry, come in for a minute, will you? Now?"

It was impossible to deduce anything from Edmunston's scratchy voice. "Sure, Rufus," he said.

Edmunston's office, as compared to Pick's, could have been located on another planet. It had heavy draperies, an Oriental rug, a richly hued conference table, dark wood paneling covered with the awards, citations, memberships, degrees, honorary degrees and photographs of the physicist with well-known people. The Director, who sat in a winged leather chair at a large polished desk with a single report on it—Pick's—was as different physically from his Deputy as he was temperamentally. Edmunston was a thin, almost birdlike figure with scrawny arms and legs and long white hair. His Deputy, towering over him, was six feet three, with shoulders rounded as though accustomed to carrying a heavy burden. The tapered waist and the arms packing his shirt sleeves suggested that the man was in good physical shape. The head, with flat ears and dark hair combed straight back, had something of the massiveness of a Roman bust. Lawrence Pick was undeniably handsome, with a square jaw, a long, straight nose, large black eyes and a wide mouth that characteristically drooped slightly at the corners when he was upset. The mouth drooped now.

Edmunston waved the engineer to a leather chair across from him, and said lazily, "Some weather, huh?"

"It's all anybody talks about."

"Can't blame them. Never seen so much rain in my life." The Director pressed a switch concealed beneath the edge of the desk. The button activated a device that created an electronic screen which blocked any listening devices aimed from the street or other buildings. The screen was used only when necessary because nobody could be positive about the effects on the health of those exposed to it. The room was also searched frequently for bugs. None had ever been found, and it was doubtful that anybody beyond a small, closed circle knew that CRISES, seemingly open, had a covert function. Nonetheless, security was invoked when certain matters came up.

Edmunston leaned forward and pushed the report back and forth on his desk. He sighed. "Larry, about this earthquake thing. Why do you always have to get so goddam excited?"

"Look, Rufus," Pick said, as though his answer were rehearsed. "The Sovs are in clear violation of the Helsinki Agreement. It specifically states that *all* earthquakes of the magnitude and intensity of this one or greater must be reported. The Sovs have said nothing. The Siberian quake was in a remote area and below the level where the international seismological network could easily pick it up. We wouldn't have known about it at all except for our own special monitoring devices, which the Sovs aren't aware of, so far as we know.

That kind of earthquake conforms exactly to the type that could have been triggered by a low megatonnage nuclear weapon detonated along a fault."

"Yes, yes," Edmunston said impatiently.

Pick knew his exposition was too detailed but went on anyway, to avoid misunderstanding. "Don't you see, Rufus? An induced earthquake like that could be a dress rehearsal for starting one undersea. It could cause a tidal—seismic—wave which could destroy naval ports like San Diego or Diego Garcia. An earthquake could be an important weapon."

"As I've said, you worry too much," Edmunston grumbled.

"I'm paid to worry, Rufus. The Sovs should have reported that quake. They didn't, and it makes me suspicious. I can't help it."

Edmunston said slowly, "And now you want to use the hot line to query them."

"Yes. In such a way that they don't understand how we got the information."

The Director blew air through a round hole he made with his mouth. "God, how I miss cigarettes. Larry, maybe I haven't learned much in all these years, but one thing I'm sure is that it's a mistake to get worked up before you have to. Look how the birthrate in Southeast Asia has suddenly started to decline after years of predictions that Spaceship Earth would crash from the sheer weight of the passengers. Take the coming famine on the Asian subcontinent. You had the whole place crazy with plans for emergency relief, and presto, there were good monsoons and no famine. Bangladesh is exporting rice now. That surprised you, didn't it?"

"I guess so." Pick had the feeling Edmunston was toying with him.

"Or, just a few months ago, you were convinced that a red

algae tide was about to kill the bottom fishes in the Gulf of Mexico and give half of Texas respiratory infections—that was you, wasn't it, Larry?"

"You know damn well it was, Rufus."

"And the infected plankton just disappeared."

"We all make mistakes," Pick said. He ran a thick hand through his dark hair. "I'd rather err on the side of safety than do nothing at all. Uncertainty isn't biased toward optimism, God knows."

"A sense of urgency isn't the same as certainty," Edmunston countered. He hesitated and said crisply, "The Soviets reported the earthquake late last night. The Science Adviser called this morning to tell me. Thank God I hadn't called *him* yet, like you wanted me to do."

Anger closed on Pick like a clamp, but he tried not to show it. "You might have told me sooner, Rufus," he answered. He was thinking that Edmunston seemed all too eager to please the Science Adviser. Did the old man want the job himself when the incumbent resigned?

The Director said easily, "I wanted to make my point. Don't you understand, Larry? The S.A. is down on us. Too much excitement, too many false alarms. I think the White House wants to close Fort Davis. It's just looking for a good excuse."

Pick protested, "But the facility is practically new! Closing it down would be a grave mistake. I don't trust the Sovs yet."

The Director shrugged. "All I know is that if we cry wolf too often, heads will roll around here." He flicked his finger toward Pick so rapidly that the motion was barely perceptible. Then, as though to soften the impact, he went on expansively, "Have a laugh or two, Larry. Get a date this weekend and go away somewhere. Jesus, if I were your age, I'd make sparks fly, I'll tell you that."

"Thanks," Pick said grumpily.

"Yessir, women are about all that count in the end. Why, you could even marry again, Larry."

"You told me that."

"I did, didn't I? Well, think over what I've said." Edmunston switched off the electronic curtain. It was a signal to leave.

2
CHAPTER

Dr. Bertram Kline was weary after ten-hour days with the computer, and the pouches under his eyes hung even lower than usual. His wife, Jody, looked at him and asked, "What's the matter? You seem upset."

"Tired is all," he said in his dry voice.

"You're always tired on Friday—that's not it. Something's bothering you. I can tell."

Kline rarely discussed his work with her. Chemistry bored lay people because they couldn't understand it, and he could not communicate the excitement he sometimes felt. He said with difficulty, "I'm a little frustrated, I guess. I've been running a series of tests and the results won't add up. I don't know why."

"Can't you be a little more specific?" she asked him patiently. He sighed and plunged in.

In 1974 the largest single experiment in science until that time took place, with an armada of 40 research ships gathered in a box of ocean and atmosphere 800 miles from West Africa. This was GATE (GARP Atlantic Tropical Experiment), spawned by GARP (Global Atmospheric Research Program). Emerging from GATE was the conclusion that the tropical seas, as one writer put it, are "the main boiler houses of the

29

whole weather machine, absorbing the sun's rays and heating the air from below. The cloud clusters are strung out like rows of smoking chimneys across the oceans."*

Then came FGGE (pronounced "Figgy"), the First GARP Global Experiment, to restudy the same quadrant of ocean and atmosphere as part of research covering the whole planet. The project involved not only ships and planes but five geostationary weather satellites, from the U.S., USSR, Japan and Europe. FGGE also used the World Weather Watch of weather stations, tied together by the hot lines and computers of the Global Telecommunications System and augmented by observations from commercial ships and planes. Balloons and automated buoys were added to the meteorological arsenal.

The FGGE results were still being analyzed in labs and computers, and so it was that a package containing plastic vials of Atlantic seawater ultimately arrived at the National Center for Atmospheric Research in Boulder, Colorado, where Kline worked as a chemist, studying the relation between pollutants and trace gases in the atmosphere and the topmost layer of the sea. The samples, taken the summer before, had arrived belatedly because, in the manner of science, somebody had neglected to send them.

Kline had worked with the water a full week, subjecting it to a battery of tests involving pressure, spectronomic analysis, atomic structure, valences, acidity, the ability to absorb various molecules, and so on, all of which required a high-speed computer, a team of young assistants and total concentration. When he had finished, Kline was uncertain of what he had found.

He told his wife, "It's, well, like a deviation so small that you can't really measure it. Long columns of numbers that seem to make sense but don't, quite. It's like something's hap-

* Nigel Calder, *The Weather Machine*, Viking, 1974, p. 49.

pening out there but I can't prove it." He sought language that Jody would understand. "I've told you the ocean breathes?" She nodded. "It inhales, or used to. I've got the funny sense it's started to exhale."

He looked so serious that she tried to make a joke of it. "Wouldn't something that inhales have to exhale, sooner or later?"

He smiled sketchily. "Say, I hadn't thought of it that way. Only . . ." The fragile smile crumpled.

"Only?"

He bent his head and sat limply. "Jody, I'm imagining things, terrible things. Dead algae. Dead plankton. Dead fish, billions of them, their carcasses strewing the sea, stinking up the world. Dead . . ."

She watched him with alarm. "Bert! I'm worried about you. I'm afraid you're getting your old trouble back. It's been a dozen years. Overwork . . ."

"It's not that," he said sullenly. "This could be real. But I can't get a fix on it. It's too subtle, and I'm not good enough."

"Not good enough! You're the best there is." She went on insistently, "You've got to tell somebody who'll understand you. I won't have you sit on this, whatever it is."

"Who can I tell? I can't prove it and without proof nobody will believe me. The implications *are* unbelievable. Maybe you're right. Maybe it's me."

"No. Share it with others. There must be somebody you can share it with. Think."

He said with reluctance, "There's an organization in Washington that might listen, I guess."

"Good," she said. "Write a report and we'll mail it tonight. With luck it'll get there Monday."

31

3
CHAPTER

NOTHING IS GAINED in blaming the luckless victims in Wild-wood Homes for the calamity that grim Sunday. They didn't create the storm the media described again and again as "freak," nor did they build the cheap, cellarless frame houses that offered pathetic protection when the funnel roared over the treetops and probed the ground.

Still, though late and confusing, warnings had been issued for central Virginia, including the town of Huntsboro. Had the residents of Wildwood Homes listened, passed the word and found refuge in either the nearby church or the school as instructed; had they observed in their own homes the most elementary precautions, like opening the windows a crack as a safeguard against the precipitous drop in barometric pressure a tornado brings, or gone to the center of the room or even better, a closet, more than fifty lives might have been saved.

They might have been saved anyway if the tornado had deviated by only a short distance. The homes in Dellwood Estates, directly across the street, were older, more expensive, and better constructed; they had cellars where most of their occupants went, needlessly as it turned out, for the storm didn't knock down so much as a TV antenna in that section.

Those in Dellwood who chose to risk a sudden turn by the tornado were rewarded by a spectacular if ghastly scene.

One of the observers, Rick Stewart, a thirty-five-year-old proprietor of a drugstore, unoriginally described the tornado's sound as "like a fleet of big jet planes." Cheryl Conner, a housewife in her twenties, said the roar was "what I imagine an erupting volcano must make." Tuffy Beccero, a trained nurse whose skills were vital during the emergency, reported, "I never heard a noise like that and pray I don't again." To twelve-year-old Pinky Fleet, "It whirred like the devil's top."

None of the witnesses had seen a tornado except in pictures, and they were astonished by the amplitude of the deep growl and by the forward speed, estimated at 40 mph, with which the one-legged giant raced toward the huddled houses until it seemed to fill the sky. Being the stuff of clouds, a twister is white until it touches down and becomes dark from the dirt and debris it sucks up, including, in this case, houses. The storm struck the Wildwood section at 4:49 P.M.

The weather had been perfect for a tornado. Warm and wet air, the result of the unusual heat wave hovering over the South, had moved in quickly from the Atlantic where it met the cold dry atmosphere just arriving over the mideastern seaboard. Physical laws were followed: the warm air, attempting to rise, met cold air above that refused to let it escape. A high-speed spin resulted. The warm moisture condensed into heavy clouds from which the whirling column reached for the ground.

As early as the day before, satellite photos of the two weather fronts had been studied at the National Severe Storms Forecast Center in Kansas City, Kansas, and at the National Weather Service in Camp Springs, Maryland, both part of the National Oceanic and Atmospheric Administration (NOAA).

Given the time of year—too late, normally, for tornadoes—and the fact that the area was not associated with tornadoes, nothing worse than severe thunderstorms was expected. Only when instrumented balloons penetrated the advancing wet air on Sunday morning did the surprised meteorologists realize how warm this layer was. Even so, tornado probability seemed low, and no action was taken until barometric pressure dropped sharply over parts of Virginia, Maryland and Delaware. That signal could not be ignored; it resulted in a tornado watch at 1 P.M. By then, cloud cover had thickened so as to interfere with further identification from satellites and Washington-based radar. Localities were on their own.

At Huntsboro, the warning, received by teletype at the police station, was broadcast to the town's two patrol cars, and at the local radio station, WHUN, where disc jockey Andy Braden periodically put it on the air. At about 3:15 Braden's phone rang. The caller was the county's volunteer Civil Defense Director, Burton Dickson, who had been using his home as a command post, placing and receiving calls about the possible tornado. Nothing had been sighted until moments before when Tinker Wheeler, a farmer who grew hothouse tomatoes, reported in. Wheeler swore that grapefruit-size hailstones had demolished two of his greenhouses. More importantly, the farmer claimed to have seen an ominous funnel sticking out of a cloud, as though it were giving birth. That put the tornado, if such it was, less than ten miles away.

Urgency edged Dickson's voice. "Can you broadcast that right now? And keep broadcasting?" Dickson gave Braden instructions on what to do in a tornado, and Braden put them on the air as well. Hoping he had more listeners than usual, he repeated the message until the power failed and the station went off the air.

The speed of a tornado's inner or rotary winds is unknown, since instruments have not withstood them, but 550 mph is cited in the literature. Whatever the exact figure, a tornado is the most violent storm on earth. (Hurricanes release more energy but over a much larger area.) That year, 1,247 had already struck the continental U.S., making the Huntsboro twister number 1,248. When the year ended, 1,309 tornadoes had touched down; before that, the record year was 1974, when over 1,200 tornadoes occurred.

But that day the only cipher mattering was one—a single tornado that broke the dreams of many. The storm skirted the virtually empty downtown area and with a furious outcry bore down on the Wildwood section, whose residents were mostly home. Rocking crazily in the premature darkness, the tornado turned black from the dirt that whirled inside. At the housing development's edge the storm seemed to hesitate, pivoting on its one leg, and then listed forward like a tree about to fall.

Despite the warnings carried by the police, the radio and word of mouth, people did little to prepare, and some did not know of the tornado's existence at all until the great grinding cry announced it. But when the storm came it was too late to seek refuge in school or church. Something in the American attitude toward private property and the protection of one's own home, and perhaps resentment toward more fortunate neighbors, would have forbidden the Wildwood inhabitants from sheltering themselves in Dellwood right across the street —if indeed the imperative to seek safety had been felt. But people had no such impulse. Interviews conducted later by a sociologist proved that they refused to believe that the storm was a threat to *them*—to others, maybe, but not *them*. In fact, the initial response of many was to go outside and watch.

When the tornado, crackling with lightning, resumed its tottering march, and whole houses disappeared inside its maw, people moved fast, but no time remained for precautions such as to place mattresses on the floor and crawl beneath them, or to open windows to equalize the pressure drop. One of the first homes in the storm's path belonged to a barber named Frank Kuhn, who ran outside when he heard the faint din and returned immediately. His three children—six, eight and eleven —still watched "The Flintstones" on TV, while Jessie, his wife, put a pie in the oven. Kuhn shouted at her, pulled the children to the floor and grabbed a table leg. The roar came, windows burst, walls buckled, and seconds later the structure no longer existed: every wall was down and twisted pipes bubbled. The furniture had been destroyed too. Frank still had the table leg but the table had disappeared. His arm was broken. The screaming children escaped serious injury but the heap on the floor was Jessie, a piece of wood impaled in her head.

A few houses away, young Billy Harris ran outside, ignoring the cries of his eight-months-pregnant mother, who couldn't move fast enough. Billy flew through the air and vanished into the vortex, his arms and legs threshing about, almost as if he were trying to swim. His hair was straight and his mouth open in a scream that couldn't be heard. The last anyone saw of him was when a bolt of lightning lit up the tornado's cone.

The mother remained unharmed but a beam fell on her husband, killing him instantly. The dog whimpered safely in the debris, helped by a low center of gravity.

The storm made effortless ruin of whatever it encountered. The awesome power can be conveyed by the fate of the family that took refuge in their car. Had they left the windows open a crack, they might have been saved: when the windshield shattered, an adult and two children were pulled into it and battered to death. Several people, unwise enough to stay outside to take pictures, or to try to put the unforgettable sound on tape, were killed by flying objects, or crushed and even dismembered, like the elderly man who was decapitated; the head was never recovered. But it was hardly safer inside the houses: exploding gas burned a woman alive and another was dragged by windy arms until her stomach ripped open.

Cooking implements, Levitz furniture, bicycles, lawn mowers, suitcases, TV antennas, toys, curtains, curtain rods, books, glassware, dishes—sucked from their usual places, the appurtenances of life became dangerous, capable with the storm's fury behind them of putting out eyes, breaking bones, tearing soft flesh. Where could people hide from the very air? The tornado, with its frightful roar, destroyed the development that had been known as Wildwood, though there had hardly been anything wild about the place until that moment. As the storm departed, witnesses attested, the sky turned a brilliant green.

The tornado raged off to the countryside, where it leveled several more houses and caused additional fatalities before at last subsiding. Within the six-block area of Wildwood, nothing worth saving remained. They talked briefly of rebuilding the place, but in the end the structures were bulldozed and the area became a park. That, as a sort of chance result, was of itself welcomed by the people of Dellwood. The treeless, lawned expanse across the street offered them a clear view of the hills. The following summer they could expect cool breezes to blow over empty land.

4
CHAPTER

FOLLOWING THE NOTION Edmunston had put in his head, Lawrence Pick spent the weekend resolutely attempting to have a good time. He telephoned a woman he knew and set off with her in his old compact, bound for nowhere in particular. If you don't know where you're going, any road will take you there, he thought dejectedly, but he was determined to have *fun* for a change.

The pursuit of pleasure stranded them at a garage for two hours when the car broke down. A seaside resort 100 miles south of Washington sounded perfect for long romantic walks on the beach, but abnormally high tides left no sand to walk on, and, it being nearly winter, the shops were closed. At last they located a second-rate motel. The only nearby restaurant was dark, and after driving endlessly in a downpour, they settled on a diner and hamburgers. Pick had brought a bottle of whiskey, and back at the motel they gamely tried to party.

She was, he felt sure, as glad to be rid of him as he was of her when they said goodbye on Sunday.

The next morning, when Pick turned on the TV, the bland-faced weatherman was talking of a tornado that had struck the afternoon before in central Virginia, not too far from where he had been. ". . . claimed fifty-four lives in all. Rescue workers still combed the wreckage this evening but the task is virtually completed. That storm was a freak in several respects. It came very late in the year for a tornado, and there is no record of a tornado ever having hit that particular section of Virginia before. A tornado watch had been in effect but the storm struck an area somewhat different than the Weather Service anticipated. It was very severe. The tornado raced along for about five miles and vanished as quickly as it had come. Luckily, heavily populated areas were spared, with the exception of a crowded development, where most of the casualties were."

Jesus, thought Pick, watching the footage. The violence of which nature was capable never failed to awe him.

On Monday mornings Pick took stock of the world. At 9:30 sharp, the heads of the various departments at CRISES met in the small auditorium on the ground floor, with a security guard posted outside, and one by one rose to discuss the most pressing problems before them and the countermeasures they recommended. It was not just for movie stars to be temperamental; so were these men and women, leading scientists all. As Deputy Director, Pick had to be tactful if he disagreed, but with his unobtrusive manner, logical mind and impeccable information, he usually succeeded in winning the others over.

Upstairs, he went through a pile of papers Gwen had assembled. CRISES served as a clearinghouse for advanced scientific information of every sort; the organization encouraged experts to send in their ideas and theories, no matter how farfetched they seemed. It was for this reason that an airmail special delivery letter from Colorado was in the stack.

The name Bertram Kline was familiar enough to command Pick's immediate attention. The NCAR chemist explained that

39

he had just run a test series on sea samples from the tropical Atlantic, and was concerned that a subtle and mysterious change in oceanic chemistry might be taking place.

In his brief report, Kline noted (needlessly for Pick) that the oceans absorb about half the excess carbon dioxide in the atmosphere—excess because industrial activity was constantly adding CO_2 to the air as a result of the burning of fossil fuels. Kline's research suggested that, instead of accepting the gas, the sea had begun returning it to the atmosphere.

Kline was tentative to the point of apology, and Pick would probably have dismissed the notion as absurd had it not been for the chemist's reputation for scrupulous accuracy. Even so, his theory had no real basis that Pick could see.

There were other reports too—like one from a University of Southern California disaster sociologist named R. Havu who had investigated why Californians were failing to respond to a new earthquake-warning system. Havu suggested that people had lost faith in science and scientists. Turning their backs on rationalism, they took refuge in meditation and mysticism. Immersed in inner, not outer, space, they were obsessed with themselves. Pick agreed and thought about Havu, "Good man."

Later that day, as also happened every Monday, Pick would meet with Edmunston to review the reports and decide which, if any, merited attention. He was about to write his comments on a buff sheet when the intercom buzzer sounded and his secretary said, "Mr. Blake is here."

"Who?"

"Mr. Benjamin Blake, from the Weather Service. We made an appointment, remember?" Gwen whispered.

Pick recalled something about an excitable young man. He glanced at his watch; it was almost lunchtime and he was hungry. "Okay," he said reluctantly.

Blake was of medium height and weight, with brown hair and brown eyes. In his tenor voice he asked needlessly, "Dr. Pick? I'm Benjamin Blake. When I called on Friday, I asked for a senior scientist, and they switched me to your office. I didn't know until right now that you're the Dep–p–p–uty," he stammered.

"Well, I am," Pick said with a small smile.

"I didn't mean *that* senior. I meant somebody lower down. I could talk to someone else if you'd prefer. . . ."

"Take a chair, please." The engineer pointed and sat down himself. "You're with the Weather Service?"

"Junior climatologist," said Blake. He still had a little acne. Pick put him at about twenty-two.

"Is it Mister or Doctor Blake?" Pick inquired.

Blake shifted and said regretfully, "Mister. I'm just out of graduate school. I only have a Master's degree, with honors. I'd have gone on if there were scholarship money around in my field. But I'll get my Ph.D. someday. If I had it now, maybe they'd listen. As it is, I'm going over people's heads."

"Understood. It happens all the time. Anything you say will be confidential," Pick replied as he studied the nervous young man. Blake seemed intelligent, but what did he have to say? Nothing of importance, surely. Scientists could delude themselves as easily as others about the value of information they possessed.

"Actually, I'm with the Air Resources Lab," Blake went on. "I read a report . . . Maybe I'd better start over. We have a weathership—we used to have several of them before Congress cut the budget—called *Oceanographer*. This fall it was in the tropical Atlantic doing routine tests—"

"Where?" Pick asked sharply.

"The tropical Atlantic," Blake repeated, looking confused. "About midway between Africa and Brazil."

41

"Wasn't that the location of the Figgy work carried out last summer?"

"Figgy was conducted a little nearer to Dakar," Blake said with authority. He waited, and when the engineer failed to reply, continued, "Anyway, a routine test on the content of atmospheric carbon dioxide just above the sea surface was performed. It isn't the kind of test that's done very often because the results never vary except in the long term, only . . . only this time they . . . That's why I'm here, because my b–b–b–boss, his name is Dr. Polchak, doesn't take the findings seriously. He thinks the sudden CO_2 increase was due to undersea volcanic activity. So did the shipboard m–m–m–meteorologist." Blake fell silent, as if trying to get himself under control.

"And you?"

"I think the numbers are too high to be explained that way," Blake protested.

"Why?" Pick said. He was leaning forward now, his big hand resting on the pile of reports that contained Kline's.

"I know it sounds nutty, but I've always been interested in atmospheric CO_2." The tone turned confessional. "I used to write science fiction, or tried to. You know, a runaway greenhouse effect is just about the only really conceivable way the world *could* end, so I tried to make a story about it, but I wasn't able to figure out a manner in which the human race could survive, so I was minus a narrator and I didn't know how to finish the story. I'm sorry—I shouldn't be going on like this. Anyway, the greenhouse effect *is* interesting when you build in manmade thermal pollution due to the consumption of fossil fuels, and I got to know a lot about it. When I get my Ph.D. that'll be my subject. I'm working on my thesis now. Anyway, it seemed to me those numbers were on the suspicious side. There could be a CO_2 buildup limited to the tropics. I've gone over the literature and there's no reason to think such a thing couldn't happen. A CO_2 buildup like that might cause a heat pocket which could account for the high-pressure heat the Southeast's been having, and some of the other crazy weather the country's had. I told that to Polchak, but he only smiled. In fact, he laughed."

In Pick's brain, the conclusions of Kline and young Blake fused as though welded by an acetylene torch. A too-acidic ocean gives up CO_2. The gas causes a heat pocket. The result is crazy weather, like the late-season tornado. Was it possible? And then what? He said carefully, "How can the tropics be heating up when northern latitude temperature seems to be falling?"

Blake replied lamely, "Could there be cooling in the temperate zones and heating in the tropics all at once? The cold winters—1976-7, for instance—could be isolated phenomena."

"Quite a theory," Pick said with a feigned chuckle. "Can you support it?"

Blake's voice was alarmed. "No, but I might be able to model it with a computer."

"You can model anything on a computer with the proper assumptions, can't you?" Pick replied. "Can you suggest anything at all in the way of irrefutable physical proof?"

"No."

"Are you suggesting that, because of the so-called CO_2 pocket, North American weather has been worse than it's been elsewhere?"

"I guess so."

"Can you explain that?"

"No."

"There you are," Pick sighed. "No, in the absence of other evidence it seems to me that your boss is undoubtedly right—undersea volcanic activity caused an upwelling of CO_2."

"But the amount . . ."

"How many parts per million did the report show?" Pick asked, and Blake told him. "I don't think that's significant by itself," the engineer said with a frown. "Oh, by the way, have you told anyone else about your idea?"

"Only Dr. Polchak," Blake said, lowering his head.

Pick's tone turned fatherly. "Good. Well, I don't think it's worth worrying about. But let me know if anything else turns up about this. Oh, do you happen to have a copy of the CO_2 report for my files? In confidence, of course."

With obvious reluctance Benjamin Blake pulled an envelope from his inside jacket pocket. "It's a thermocopy. You won't . . . if P–P–Polchak knew . . ."

"It's safe with me."

He thanked the junior climatologist for coming in and walked him to the door. Blake seemed half relieved and half disappointed not to be in on the ground floor of an important scientific event.

Back at his desk, Pick ran a hand through his hair. As he reviewed the situation, the edges of his mouth pointed down. In the matter of a very few minutes a potentially vital matter had presented itself.

Many responsible scientists believed that global cooling began about 1940 and was continuing. Another group, smaller but equally responsible, thought the earth's thermometer would point in the other direction. The disagreement ultimately resulted from different opinions on the effect of atmospheric carbon dioxide. Though CO_2 existed in the air only as a trace gas, it impeded long or infrared radiation from bouncing back into space after it had reached the earth. CO_2 acted like a greenhouse, in which solar energy penetrated the glass and was trapped there, making the greenhouse warmer than the air outside. This was the so-called "greenhouse effect," a term

44

coined by a British scientist, Tyndall, in the 1860's. CO_2 was a vital atmospheric element because it kept the planet warm.

But the combustion of chemical fuels put more and more CO_2 into the air. A combination of growing manmade heat, and increasing heat trapped by the CO_2 blanket, could make mercury in thermometers rise that much higher and faster. No one could really say by how much. That atmospheric CO_2 was rising in quantity had been amply documented. If the CO_2 blanket became too dense, too much infrared radiation would be retained and the world would become hotter—"hothouse earth," it had been said.

If the CO_2 density was on the rise, it would begin in the tropics because warm water gives up CO_2 more easily than cold. But, in the absence of other evidence, why tell Edmunston? Why risk further loss of credibility? And even if the climate was in trouble, it might be centuries before the effects were felt. Why *me?* asked Lawrence Pick. Let the goddam human race take care of itself. He had a good job, so why jeopardize it? Find a wife and stop worrying. . . . Pick was determined not to say a single word to Edmunston about the possibility, which he then judged infinitely small, of a climate change.

Suddenly he grabbed the phone and called the Director, canceling their afternoon meeting. Pleading a toothache, he changed it to the following day.

5
CHAPTER

THE FIRST LAW OF SECRECY declares that the fact of secrecy itself should be a secret. It was a poorly kept secret that the Army's maximum security telecommunications center at Fort Johnson, 30 miles from Washington, had been determined "overage" and phased out, but a well-kept one that a new tenant occupied the premises.

The new occupant was called CRISES Operations Program, or COP. Some of the handful of scientists privy to COP's existence declared that the facility should be declassified because it represented a remarkable advance in the conceptualization of the world. If tourists posed a problem, admit the press at least, they said. Additional traffic, came the response, would interfere with the controlled temperature and humidity conditions required for the operation of ILLIAC VII, one of the world's largest computers. What about an observation gallery? Too expensive to construct. Why not open COP to concerned scientists, at least? The "hole," said Lawrence Pick, who ran the place, was too crowded already. No. No. No.

Those who argued for opening the hole revealed at once that they failed to grasp why electronic surveillance devices, armed soldiers and dogs guarded it. COP's main purpose was to monitor possible ecological modification, inadvertent or hostile. It was meant to be a place where vital decisions could be made in secret, without the pressure of publicity.

COP performed several ongoing missions that could never be openly discussed. One was called COMPWATCH, for Computer Watch. Either through ordinary networks or secret tie lines, ILLIAC "eavesdropped" on major computers in the U.S., unknown to their owners, to provide COP with environmental information that might not have been disseminated, because of secrecy, caution, ignorance or ineptitude. Also, ILLIAC was actually able to interfere with the operations of other computers to change their results, though this capability had never been used.

The overriding reason for COP's secrecy was that it monitored possible Soviet activities in weather and climate modification. Despite the treaty banning geophysical warfare, it was felt necessary to monitor the Russians for violations (as the Russians doubtless monitored the U.S.). Using Continuous Astrophysical Surveillance Satellites (CASS) masked as weather satellites, COP maintained a 24-hour vigil against Adverse Environmental Modification (AEM) and a Surprise Environmental Attack (SEA). From the rainmaking practiced by the U.S. in Indochina, ideas about weather warfare had become sophisticated. The potential weapons included: starting fiery cyclones called "fire storms," making rain acidic to knock out equipment, forming or intensifying fog, bringing about prolonged droughts by "stealing" rain, causing seismic waves, punching holes in the ozone layer with laser beams to increase radiation, manipulating electric properties in the atmosphere so as to interfere with normal electrical processes of the brain and bring about disorientation and derangement. There seemed no end to what might be done, and some kinds

47

of weather warfare might be slow and insidiously difficult to detect.*

The exit had been specially constructed; the numbered sign gave no indication where it went. Those who took it by accident quickly returned to the expressway because the road seemed to lead nowhere in particular. There was a bridge, forbiddingly strait, followed by narrow pavement without a dividing line. After a short distance Pick came in sight of a hill. The hill was an accident of nature. Its sides rising steeply to a rounded top, the hill almost resembled a human head without features. A sign on the high fence said redundantly, "Ft. Davis. U.S. Government Property. Access Prohibited to All But Authorized Personnel. No Trespassing. Keep Out. Warning: This Fence Is Electrified." A jagged red line represented electricity.

Pick stopped at the gate as he always did when Haggerty was on duty. Sergeant Haggerty was from Boston, where Pick had studied, so they had a kind of kinship. The engineer rolled down his window and asked, "What's new, Bud?"

"Not a hell of a lot, Dr. Pick," Haggerty said. "Did you hear what the wind did to that big building in Boston?"

"You mean the John Hancock Tower, Bud? No. I must have missed that."

"Blew out half the windows again. Second time since summer. Seems like there's more wind in Boston than usual, which is saying something," Bud said.

"Well, take it easy."

He proceeded up a sharply winding road and reached a parking slot designated as his. Before him was a squat build-

---

* COP evolved out of the Department of Defense's project "Nile Blue" which, in 1972, had a budget of $2,587 million to develop computer models of the world's weather, partly to detect climate modification by other countries for hostile and non-hostile purposes.

ing, invisible from below. Inside, he went to a small, plainly furnished office and changed from sports clothes into a trim, white, freshly pressed uniform.

Next to his desk stood a computer terminal on a slender metal stalk, and with it the engineer began the tedious task of interrogating the giant computer. ILLIAC VII was constantly fed data from every source, which it cross-referenced and tried to analyze. The machine "knew" so much about the physical world that someone at COP described it as "the mind of the globe." Pick began to type on the keyboard. Blake had said that the tropical heat pocket might be capable of causing unstable, volatile weather farther north, but suppose the weather had been screwy in China or other faraway places? If so, that could have nothing to do with a patch of warmth in the tropical Atlantic, and so much for the junior climatologist's suspicions.

Boiled down, Pick's first question to the computer was: Can you detect a pattern in recent meteorological trends indicating that North American weather is worse than weather in the rest of the world?

ILLIAC was equipped to answer by printout, speech or both, so that a user could listen to the machine while engaged in other activities. Pick used audio. A breathy, staccato female voice said, "Wait."

Wait, Pick thought irritably. *Women always make you wait.* He stared moodily at the terminal and said aloud in a tone that almost conveyed fondness for the mechanical contraption, "Come on. Come on."

As if on cue the computer said, "Positive. U.S.–Canadian weather more inclement than most other places. Comparisons follow. . . ."

Pick typed: "Stop." Jesus, could it be true? Next he asked, in effect, is the weather of Mexico abnormal? And learned that it wasn't. But that didn't mean much, he decided. Mexico might be too far south to be affected.

His mind turned next to the Soviet Union. Although mostly convinced that Russia was unable to affect the weather over the United States, Pick felt a compulsion to investigate. He proceeded indirectly, aware that if ILLIAC had already learned of such a capability, the machine would have reported it. First he asked: How can U.S.–S.U. be compared weatherwise?

If Russia had been experiencing the mildest, most beneficent winter in history, that might have been reason for concern, but the Soviet Union was having a cold winter. The Sovs wouldn't mess up their own weather to ruin ours. Scratch that idea, he told himself.

What emerged was that North America above Mexico seemed to be having an exceptionally difficult winter. Why? Did it mean anything? Pick then addressed the issue frontally: he instructed ILLIAC to search itself for even the smallest hints that long-run meteorological changes might be in the making.

"Search completed. Evidence follows. Retreat of Northwest Icelandic ice pack unusual for this time of year. Populations of the dog flea (*Cteno cephalides canis*) and the cat flea (*Cteno cephalides felis*) species, common throughout the U.S., reached unusually high levels in the southeastern states of Florida, Georgia, North Carolina, Alabama and Louisiana, also in east Texas. Infestation attributed to unusually mild winters over the last decade. Dog and cat fleas can cause skin irritation but do not constitute a serious public health hazard. Recommended extermination procedure . . ."

"Stop." The computer lacked discrimination. It didn't know when to quit. Persisting, he asked, Had there been any undersea volcanic activity in the area *Oceanographer* had been when the CO_2 test was conducted? Negative, the computer pronounced. Then Pick inquired if rises in atmospheric CO_2 had been reported. Affirmative, the computer said—minor rises around the tropical Atlantic. But the information came from small foreign weather stations which the machine didn't consider reliable.

How American of the computer, Pick thought. Well, the evidence remained insubstantial. It would be hard to make the Director of CRISES listen, harder probably to convince politicians and the common man, assuming of course that the CO_2 buildup were real. He began placing a series of telephone calls. Careful always to state that CRISES was engaged in a routine study, he contacted the U.S. weather establishment—the National Disaster Warning Program (NADWARN), NCAR, NOAA Environmental Research Laboratory, also in Boulder, the Environmental Studies Program at Dartmouth, the River Forecast Center in Kansas City and many others. He tried to learn if anyone had stumbled on evidence or entertained the thought of a long-term climate change toward heat; no one had, and Pick did not communicate his fears.

The engineer was about to return to Washington when the phone rang. It was from a technician named Baxter working below. Pick had ordered that any unusual meteorological activity be reported to him at once. "A storm's forming in the tropical Atlantic. Just thought I'd let you know," Baxter said.

"I'll come down," Pick replied. He went to the massive steel doors of one of two elevators in the low-ceilinged hallway, inserted a long metal rod into an aperture, and the doors sprang open. The car dropped him six stories into the hill with a whoosh.

In the huge chamber known as the "hole" the globe turned

slowly, exerting on Pick a hypnotic fascination, drawing him toward it. Over forty feet in diameter, the ball was a perfect replica of the planet as it existed that very moment—bright from interior illumination where the sun shone, shadowy where the sun was setting, dark where it was night. Three paper-thin layers of plastic in slightly different pastels—representing the ionosphere, the stratosphere and the troposphere—covered it, and simulated clouds, representing real cloud cover wherever the weather satellites reported it, hung in the plastic sky. Beneath was the earth—snowy poles, oceans, continents, deserts, mountains, lakes, forests, grassy plains, rivers. . . . Lights marked major cities. Cross-hatching the globe were maintenance rungs of almost invisible Lucite.

Tiers surrounded the ersatz earth—metal platforms with desks and tables, each sectored according to function: "Population Growth," "Resource Availability," "Food Supplies," "Rainfall," and so on. Each sector had movable panels on which information could be made to appear from ILLIAC VII, a sprawling monster of steel cabinets that filled the floor of the hole.

At strategic places in the huge chamber, mounted on tripods, were pencil-thin metal tubes. These were laser guns, which were among the weapons with which ILLIAC had been equipped to conduct its own defense, if necessary.

In the sector marked "Hurricanes" Pick found Baxter, a man in his middle fifties with steel eyeglasses and a mild face. In a white uniform he was punching numbers into a computer terminal and gazing owlishly at ILLIAC's response on a printout. "Well?" Pick asked.

"Dunno," Baxter replied. "That thing's come into existence from nowhere—just like that. It may have hurricane potential. Want to look at her?"

"Sure."

Baxter spoke to a box. "Hansen, let's look at the disturbance again. Give me a closeup, too."

Attached to the wall between the semicircular layers of tiers was a control booth with a white-suited technician inside. The man contained in glass leaned forward and punched commands on the console. Abruptly the globe turned and stopped, with the western hemisphere facing them. A small mass lay in mid-ocean north of the equator. Simultaneously the ceiling became a screen that showed a magnified version of the storm, in color, as taken by satellite. It had whirling white fringes like the hair of an angry old woman. Inside were dark clouds with red lightning.

"Is there a projected course?" Pick asked.

"No. So far it's barely moved, but if it maintained its present direction and built up it might hit Florida as a full-fledged hurricane, though it's awfully late in the year."

"Any Sov naval activity out there?"

Both the Soviets and the Americans had theories for aiming hurricanes but they hadn't been thoroughly tested because the Helsinki treaty made such activity illegal, except by international agreement, but maybe the Sovs . . . Baxter, looking dubious, gave the order, and black crosses of various sizes appeared in the oceans of the western hemisphere; none was anywhere near the storm.

"The Soviets have nothing to do with it," Baxter said softly.

"I like to cover all the bases," the engineer muttered.

In his upstairs office, he sat pondering. Conditioned as he was to distrust the Sovs, they were out of it. In a way he wished they were responsible—it would have made the situation easier to understand and deal with. But our own misuse of energy was the problem—if there was a problem.

He spent the entire night analyzing and reanalyzing the scant information he possessed. Toward dawn, the engineer

CRISES OPERATIONS PROGRAM (COP)
CRISES ASSESSMENT SCALE TABULATION (CAST)
EVENT:

Astrophysical	*Biological*	*Ecological*	*Economopolitical*
CLASS I			
(Major) fireballs, landslides, avalanches, volcanic activity, dust storms, meteorites, blizzards	(Major) insect infestations, rodent infestations, crop failures, major livestock epidemic, forest fires	Atmospheric inversions, radioactive waste leaks, oil spills, serious water pollution, explosions, major forest fires	Shortages of key minerals, prolonged strikes, assassinations, insurrections, terrorism
CLASS II			
(Major) storm surges, seismic or tidal waves, earthquakes, hurricanes, tornadoes	(Major) crop failures, famine, epidemics, overpopulation	Massive oil spills, mercury-lead-cadmium pollution	Revolutions
CLASS III			
8.6 and up.Richter scale earthquake in heavily populated area; impact of large meteor near populated place	Massive drought, massive famine, new rise in birthrate	Massive pollution, renewed H-bomb, atmospheric testing; peacetime nuclear calamity	Collapse of communism; large conventional war, nuclear blackmail, totalitarian regimes everywhere, limited nuclear war; economic collapse of the West; militaristic totalitarian regimes globally

CLASS IV

New ice age; disruption of ozone shield; other limited climate modifications	Drastic overpopulation	Release of deadly new virus without a cure	Exhaustion of conventional fuels; chemical-biological warfare; total nuclear war

CLASS V

Extensive climate modification; earth tilts on axis; supernova explodes in galaxy; impact with "black hole" took a paper and pencil and began writing columns of words, at last circling two. The words were "Condition Green."

As part of its Disaster Planning and Response (DPR), CRISES graded real and conceivable calamities in terms of their gravity. The scale ran from a Class I to a Class V crisis. Class I meant moderate importance, like a big blizzard. Class II was more serious—a crop failure or a massive oil spill. Class III meant major disruptions and/or fatalities—epidemics, a revolution in the Soviet Union, a new jump in the Asian birth-rate. Class IV warned of mass fatalities and structural social changes to cope with them, as might follow the release of a new and deadly virus for which no cure presently existed. A Class V crisis spoke of the impairment of the human ability to survive, or even of the extinction of higher forms of life.

Until then, no crisis had been graded IV, much less V.

Back in his downtown office that morning, before his meeting with Edmunston, Pick placed a call to Princeton, New Jersey, and made an appointment for the following day.

"How's the toothache?" Edmunston wanted to know that afternoon. "Lose anything?"

"No. A cavity, that's all. Rufus . . ."

"What?"

He shook his big head stubbornly. "Doesn't matter."

He was still determined to tell the Director nothing—at least not yet. Although he could feel the pressure starting in him, like a wind rising beneath dark clouds, it seemed useless to discuss the matter unless he had more evidence.

They were almost down to the bottom of the pile of reports when Pick reached the one by R. Havu on earthquake-warning response, which he summarized for Edmunston, who read as little as he could. When the Deputy cited the sociologist's conclusions—that people had lost faith in science—the Director pulled his white hair. "No, no, no," he grumbled in his scratchy voice. "I hate overcomplication. People need time to adjust to new things and that's all there is to it. They'll respond to the warning system eventually. Science will find a way to convince them."

"Science will find a way" was a favorite idea of Edmunston's, and he droned on, while Pick glanced at the next report in the stack, the one from Kline, which he had been trying to forget. Suddenly he muttered, "It just can't be true."

Edmunston, misunderstanding, replied, "That's just like you, Larry. Why, if I were as pessimistic as you, I'd pack up."

"That's not what I meant, Rufus." He found himself unable to be silent as he'd planned. "Something in one of these reports. Pieces that fall into place."

"Pieces?" Edmunston asked warily.

Pick sighed and plunged in. He summarized Kline's report, described Blake's visit and mentioned the greenhouse effect. He told of his inconclusive dialogue with ILLIAC. "A thick CO_2 blanket would cause global temperature to rise."

Edmunston nodded imperturbably. "Surely the CO_2 increase would have been noticed."

"Not necessarily. The change, if there is one, is still very small and confined to the tropics, where there's hardly any instrumentation. The weather satellites don't record surface temperatures."

The old man examined the veins on the back of his hand. "How serious is this?"

"I don't know. The world's weather could go crazy."

Edmunston winced. "Is that likely?"

"Probably not likely at all. Still, I think the potential consequences are too dangerous to ignore. I think we should look into it."

"Why don't we wait and see what happens?"

"Well, if you say so, Rufus. Still, I wonder how they'll feel a hundred years from now when they find out that people in the twentieth century knew what was coming and kept their mouths shut. They'll be a little bitter. The future's our responsibility, in your own immortal words."

Edmunston leaned forward and grumbled. "If you can't find a catastrophe to worry about for this year, you'll find one in the coming centuries. We'll talk about it, Larry, but not today. I've got enough to do. Larry, you look tired. Take a vacation. But you won't do that, will you? Let's see—I've got it." He reached into a drawer and pulled out a printed sheet. "There's a conference in Florida, starting next Monday. I'm supposed to go in my official capacity, but I don't want to. Take my place, will you? The subject is the effects of disasters on human events. Bunch of Cassandras, probably, so you'll fit in fine. They've reserved the Presidential suite for me, so use it. Lot of pretty girls in Florida. They'll be impressed by the accommodations," the old man said with a lascivious laugh.

"Rufus, I wish you'd listen."

But Edmundston reached for the button below the desktop.

6

CHAPTER

PICK'S DESTINATION IN PRINCETON was a long low structure
called the Geophysical Fluid Dynamics Laboratory, a NOAA
facility that specialized in modeling climate on a huge computer. He asked the receptionist for Harold Anderson and was
told that Dr. Anderson was giving a lecture.

Harold Anderson was a thirty-five-year-old climatologist and
computer-modeling expert, one of the best, Pick knew, having
used him as a consultant. The engineer entered and stood at
the back of the room.

Anderson, a stocky man with a ruddy face and freckles,
wearing a sports shirt and wrinkled corduroys, spoke in a
rapid high-pitched voice to several dozen scientists. "It seems
likely," he said, "the northeastern United States is in for much
colder winter weather, possibly beginning in the next few decades. In Boston, for instance, it could get down to twenty, even
thirty, below zero and it would be damn cold at Princeton, too.
As you know, the periods between ice ages appear to be about
one hundred thousand years, and that means glaciation could
begin at any time now. Here at the lab—" Anderson paused
and sipped from a glass on the lectern—"we've recently completed a new eighteen-level numerical model on the computer

59

which gives some new, and I'm afraid quite startling, data on the possibility of a snow blitz . . ."

"Snow blitz?" asked a cadaverous man with a gold tooth and a Russian accent. "This term with I am not familiar."

"Blitz. Something that happens fast. As in blitzkrieg. Our model points to the view that the ice would come fast. It wouldn't be a matter of the glaciers creeping south slowly from the Arctic over a period of twenty thousand years. Rather, maybe starting soon, snow wouldn't melt completely in the summer because it would be too cold. More snow stays next summer until you'd get permanent snow as far south as Connecticut, maybe. The process could take place in seven years or less. You could get increases of one or two feet of snow a year over Canada and the whole northern United States. Every year the snow thickens, until a layer of ice lies over the ground, gradually becoming an ice sheet."

"A *year?*" asked a startled voice that sounded English. "But agriculture would be impossible in such conditions."

"I'm afraid so. But don't worry, Nigel. The Gulf Stream ought to protect Britain." Anderson glanced at the thin man with the gold tooth. "It *could* happen in large parts of the Soviet Union."

"How long glaciation takes in your model?" the Russian inquired.

"Well, that depends how you define glaciation. As I said, you'd get permanent snow cover almost at once. Snowfall would increase as cold does. This model predicts a northeastern glacier two hundred to three hundred feet deep in less than fifty years."

"Things *can't* happen to climate that fast," objected the English scientist.

"No?" Anderson's smile signaled that a favorite example was about to be cited. "You all remember the mastodons that were found frozen in blocks of ice with unchewed buttercups in their mouths? Well, I've made some calculations here and we believe that for those animals to be frozen alive in that fashion the temperature would have to have dropped to one hundred and fifty degrees below zero in *just two seconds*. Yes, there's a way to explain that. A big bolide—meteor—strike would toss hundreds of tons of matter into the upper atmosphere, and when it returned, a huge rush of sub-freezing air would fall with it. The dust cloud would cause an ice age at once, so the mastodons didn't melt. Some disagree with that theory, I might add. Any more questions?" He glanced at Pick and said, "No? Then Dr. Hathaway will talk to you about our latest work on the relationship between the Himalayas and the monsoons. Thanks."

He stepped from the platform, spoke to several visitors and went to the engineer, holding out his hand. "Hey, Larry! You made it. Come to my office where we can talk."

As they walked down the hall, Pick said, "Give briefings often?"

"More and more. The Lab's becoming a mecca for foreign scientists. I'm bored with it and it cuts into my computer time."

"That stuff about the mastodons' quick-freeze is bullshit," Pick said.

"Maybe. Birdseye mastodons, I call them. It makes a good story." They entered Anderson's cluttered office and sat at the gray metal desk. "Well, what brings you here? You sounded mighty mysterious on the telephone yesterday."

"Can anybody hear us?" Pick glanced at the open door and Anderson got up to close it. The engineer sucked in his breath and went on, "Well, bear in mind that what I'm about to tell you is probably nonsense but just the same I want to look into it." He hesitated, wondering suddenly if Anderson

61

could be completely trusted. Anderson was ambitious to a fault and highly competitive, even for a scientist. But Pick didn't see how Anderson could misuse the information at this stage, and besides, he needed the climatologist's skill.

"What is it?" Anderson asked.

"A climate change. Only in the other direction from what you were talking about in there."

"Toward heat?" Anderson asked. "If it weren't you, Larry . . ."

"I know. I know. Just the same, the evidence for global cooling isn't totally solid. Lots dispute it."

"Yes," Anderson admitted. "And even if the cooling should start, there are things that could offset it, like increased CO_2."

"That's why I'm here," Pick said quietly. "There's evidence, scanty, I admit, that a CO_2 buildup may have begun. I wanted you to work out what the picture might look like on your computer models, using the figures I have." From his briefcase Pick took a tan folder with CRISES printed on it and handed it to Anderson. He added, "I tried to verify the situation myself but didn't get anything conclusive either way."

The climatologist accepted the folder without enthusiasm. "You sure you know what you're talking about?"

"No, that's the point," Pick said earnestly. "One more thing, Hal. You spoke in there of how fast a glacier might start. How rapidly could the climate turn hotter?"

"Well, I take the view that climate change of *any* kind can be rapid." He looked at his watch. "I'll get started on this on the weekend. I'll get others to help me. It shouldn't take long."

Pick's dark head shook emphatically. "No, this must be done in total secrecy. That's why I came in person. The thing's got to be kept under complete wraps until we understand it better."

Anderson sighed. "It'll take longer then. I'll have to work at night."

"How long? I'm in a rush."

The climatologist opened the folder and inspected the contents. "Give me ten days," he lamented.

"OK." Pick consulted his datebook and wrote on a piece of paper. "I'll be at a blah-blah convention in Miami. That's the phone number of the hotel. Call me the minute you've got something."

"Or nothing."

"Let's hope," Pick said uneasily. He watched Anderson for a moment. "Looks like you're in a hurry."

"Got a tennis game with my wife," Anderson said.

"Oh? Do you beat her?"

"Do I beat my wife?" Anderson laughed lightly. "She's pretty good but, yes, I beat her. I like to win."

PART II
THE SIGNAL

7
CHAPTER

THE CONFERENCE, HELD at the Sonesta Beach Hotel on Key Biscayne, and called "Natural Events and the Affairs of Man," attracted several hundred scientists from a broad range of disciplines—volcanists, seismologists, astronomers, climatologists, meteorologists, physicists, dendrochronologists (who measure tree rings), demographers, chemists, sociologists, historians and more.

A nutritionist attempted to substantiate a theory that only Caucasians have the enzymes to digest milk properly. When it was pointed out that the tall Watusi, in Africa, drink milk, a geneticist maintained that the Watusi had come from farther north, and originally had been white. Climate change had driven them south.

Similarly, another scientist said, what was now the Scottish people had come long ago from Egypt. Again, climate had caused the migration.

A geographer claimed that the Bering Strait land bridge, over which the forebears of the American Indians once arrived on this continent, had been 1,300 miles wide.

The need for personal achievement, said an anthropologist, had been greatest along a line marking an average temperature of 50° F. When it was argued that mean temperature varied with climate changes, the anthropologist remarked that performance also did.

A follower of Immanuel Velikovsky tried to convince dubious listeners that a collision with Mars was imminent. Adherents of the Jupiter Effect claimed that when the planets lined up in a certain way tremendous earthquakes and climate change resulted on earth because of the gravitational effect.

Others predicted a vast increase in volcanic activity that would cause extensive global cooling, citing the effect of volcanic ash girdling the globe. When Katmai erupted in Alaska in 1912, it reduced sunlight in Algeria by 20 percent. The explosion of Mount Agung in Bali in 1963 reduced sunlight in the Soviet Union by 5 percent and caused, worldwide, a mean annual temperature drop of $\frac{1}{3}°$ C. that lasted two years.

Some claimed that wars, revolutions, inventions and social change were organically related to climate. Some attributed climate modification principally to volcanic dust, others to tremendous bolide strikes, still others to reversals in the earth's magnetic poles. Some were convinced that civilizations rose and fell not out of mismanagement, fatigue, technological failures, obsolescence of basic institutions or failure of will, but because, quite simply, the climate went to pot.

As Lawrence Pick noted, the conference was to some extent misnamed, because a sizable number of scientists were not concerned with "natural" events but with inadvertent climate modification by man himself. For the first time in history, humanity had the power—through technological advances and the sheer weight of numbers—to change the climate in which we live. This was something new under the sun. Mark Twain joked that everybody talks about the weather but nobody does anything about it, but people *were* doing something about it, possibly something dangerous.

Restless, the engineer wandered from conference room to conference room, using a mimeographed sheet to check the topic and the names of the participants. He came to one conference where the subject was "Climate as a Cause of Social Unrest" and saw on the roster that one of the panelists was R. Havu. Remembering the name, he examined the dais, at which four men and a woman sat. He moved forward to read the name cards before each. Just as he identified Havu, she lifted her head. Blue eyes met his black ones. Their gazes locked until, almost reluctantly, Pick looked away.

In his first, superficial impression, R. Havu was striking rather than beautiful. She wore a baggy blouse buttoned to the neck, blond hair in a tight, unflattering bun, no makeup. She looked austere and chilly. And yet her appearance had a classic simplicity that attracted him—oval face, high cheekbones, small round mouth, straight nose, pale skin—with a fillip: R. Havu's eyes were slightly folded at the corners.

R. Havu? he wondered. What does R. stand for? What kind of name is Havu? Is she married? If so, is her husband here?

She slipped in and out of his consciousness as the day progressed, with Pick frequently cornered by earnest scientists needing funds for research projects, since CRISES was in a position to help. As he talked in hallways and at the buffet lunch, Pick watched for the youthful blonde with the strange eyes. *Where* was she?

Not at the afternoon coffee break. He thought he glimpsed her leaving the welcoming cocktail party for participants, but he wasn't sure. Bored, he left the predominantly male crowd in the ballroom and went outside. The air smelled fresh after the recycled smoke that passed for air conditioning. It was warm outdoors, extremely so for the season, almost as if summer hadn't ended.

He watched the sun drop behind long red clouds. It seemed to him that the sky had the faintest tinge of green—maybe because of the lights of Miami across the causeway. But before he could consider the question he became aware of a steady splashing from the pool behind, and turning, realized instantly that the elusive woman had miraculously swum into view. The graceful body with long hair flowing free *had* to be hers. He didn't permit himself to think; not the boldest of men when it came to women, the slightest cerebration would have made him back off. Instead, he walked to the poolside and stared down.

Havu executed a racing turn and on the lap back faced the other way. He followed, pleased by her easy movements and what he could see of her narrow shape, and he was positioned to be nearby when she turned once more. There could be no doubt now that the epicanthic eye examined him like that of a fish deciding whether to be friendly. Toward the end of the lap, the woman did a surface dive, feet straight up, toes pointed. She reappeared, treading water, directly in front of him.

"Yes, Dr. Pick?" she called.

"How did you . . . ?"

"Know your name? Everybody knows you. I even sent you a paper—not that you bothered to acknowledge it."

"Hasn't been time. I've been busy," he said apologetically. "I admired your report very much, Dr. Havu."

"Go on," she told him, splashing a little water his way. "I bet you didn't even read it."

"Bet I did!" he protested with a crooked smile. "And I agree with you that people have lost faith in science. It frightens me."

"*You* don't look like you'd be frightened of anything," she answered, appraising him. "Throw me my towel, will you? It's on the chair."

As she leveraged herself up on the poolside he tried not to

stare at her largish breasts, half exposed in the bikini. He handed her the towel with a gruff "Here."

"How did you know who *I* was?"

Pick examined his feet. "Well, I . . . ah . . . saw you on one of the panels. You're . . . ah . . . hard *not* to notice, Dr. Havu."

"I guess that's a compliment. Call me Rita."

"I'm Larry," he bumbled, adding for lack of anything else to say, "What kind of name is Havu? Is it your husband's?"

"It's my mother's maiden name, as a matter of fact. I've used it since I was a little girl, when Daddy left. Sometimes I hardly remember what my real one is. Havu's a Finnish name. My grandparents were Finnish. It's where I got . . . these." She put her fingers to her epicanthic eyelids. "Lots of Finns have them. We've got a Mongol strain, alone among Europeans."

"Havu's kind of exotic," he said, staring at her face.

The woman blinked rapidly and went on, "I hate people who make puns on it. 'Hav-u a cigarette? Hav-u the time?' Christ, I've heard jokes like that all my life. People aren't very original sometimes." In a seemingly unconscious gesture she extended her hand as she rose, and he helped her. She clung to his fingers a little longer than necessary.

He would try to tell himself afterward that nothing had happened, or, if something had, it could be accounted for by a breeze gusting off the warm Atlantic, but right then it was as if the tall, slender, nearly naked woman who faced him from not a yard away exuded heat. Her skin reddened briefly as if an electric current passed through her. It was the same with him—a sensation that his face had flushed, that his own body gave off a bolt of heat. But that was imagination, wasn't it?

The engineer released her hand and stepped back, wonder-

71

ing if Rita had experienced what he had, but her face was impassive. She went on quickly, "Did you want to say something to me?"

"What? Oh, sure. Are you enjoying the conference, Dr. Havu? Rita, I mean."

"Enjoy? I'm on a sabbatical so I had time to come. I rather wish I hadn't. Maybe it's interesting in places but I don't exactly *enjoy* hearing about disasters. Today I went for a long walk." She paused. "Aren't you one of those people who cry doom?"

"Where did you hear that?" he asked.

"The men talk. I don't think it's an accident that most participants are male, do you? Men love grand speculations. It must give them a sense of power. Women are tidier in their thinking. They deal in neater worlds."

"I'm supposed to be a prophet of doom?" he said patiently.

"I guess so. You're supposed to have a lot of theories . . ." She faltered, as if afraid of becoming too personal, and went on, "I think men become fixated on their theories because they become part of their personalities. Giving up a pet theory would be like giving up part of themselves. Men have a predisposed way of looking at things. See how your mouth droops at the edges? Anybody could tell how you figure things will turn out—bad. Don't you understand? Theories become self-affirming. . . ."

"*Are* you married?"

"No. And I don't want to be." She examined the horizon swiftly. "What a glorious sunset . . . so hot for this time of year. . . ." The eyes returned to him. "What about you? Are you single, too?"

It wasn't like her, she said, and he believed her because it wasn't like him either. He didn't pick people up or stumble

72

aimlessly into romance. Didn't wander into it period. Hadn't been in love since clinking bracelets, didn't think it would ever happen again. But, having wakened in the half-light of Florida dawn, he lay there listening to her breathing, momentarily uncertain in his euphoric confusion whose room they had gone to last night—his, he decided, because they were in a suite, yes, the one reserved for Edmunston. (Wouldn't the old man be delighted at how *this* had turned out!) But he had no doubt about the reality of what he felt for her.

They had no reason for furtiveness and yet an austere scientific conference seemed altogether the wrong arena for ardor, even if they had inclined to public displays. With others they remained their professional selves, she detached and brisk, he dry, skeptical, laconic. Nightfall mercifully relieved them of their roles. That went on one whole day, after which they stopped attending the sessions altogether.

"Rita," he said to her in bed, "maybe it's me—I'm not so goddam experienced when you get right down to it—but I— can I speak out? I never had a woman like you, Rita. I didn't know a woman could be so, well, skillful."

She smiled prettily. "You bring out the best in me."

"It's more than that." His dark face turned suspicious. "*You* must have had a lot of experience," he said, as if in accusation.

Rita seemed surprised. "Me? I like men—I don't deny that. I'm sure I've had a normal number of affairs, but nothing abnormal, I assure you," she said.

"What's normal?" he grumbled jealously. "How many?"

"Not very many in the long run."

"How about the short run?"

"Oh, shut up."

Pick learned then that Havu's rather dowdy way of dressing and cool outward manner were a pose she had adopted long ago, having come to distrust the attentions her looks earned.

Rita had been raised in Los Angeles, where her divorced mother had failed as an actress. For years her mother had carted the little blonde with unusual eyes to auditions and beauty contests. Rita might have succeeded in show business if she hadn't hated it so much, but she had a choice not normally open to beauty-contest winners. She had a good brain and could enter academic life. She did, mostly on scholarships, she said.

Skilled at faking, she deliberately underplayed her looks and cultivated a chilly exterior so that men would leave her alone to work. The aloof Havu, twenty-eight years old now, could wait for a man who respected her intelligence. She confessed, "I was starting to be afraid that the *other* me—the one I think of as *Dr.* Havu—was taking over, like Dr. Jekyll and *Mrs.* Hyde. You know." He stroked the blond hair that hung to her shoulders. "But not any more!"

"Well, you've freed me up too."

Sitting on her trim haunches, she glanced down at him. "Yes, you're not exactly a ball of fire outwardly either. How did you become so serious?"

He answered uncomfortably, "I always have been, I guess. Ever since I was a kid. I felt—it sounds silly to say it."

"Say it."

"Well, I'm from the sticks. Rural Pennsylvania. My folks had a farm. Raised corn and hay . . ."

"Are they still there?"

"No. When my father died, my mother went to live with my brother in Philadelphia. He's a doctor. He didn't want to live on the farm and I didn't either, so mother sold it. My God, when I think how different we kids are from our parents, and from the people of Sonestown, where the farm was."

"Sonestown? Never heard of it. How big is Sonestown?"

"A couple of hundred. At least it used to be. Anyway, you

never completely escape the past. The people of the area were religious. So was I. I thought about being a Presbyterian minister once."

"Really?" she said with a look of surprise. "Are you still a believer?"

"I guess not," he said slowly. "I can't square that kind of faith and science. But I'm sure the influence remains, so maybe I'm a believer without knowing it. You get a sort of save-the-world complex." He hesitated, embarrassed to talk about himself. "You feel special somehow, like you were singled out to perform an unusual duty. I realize it's ridiculous, but sometimes I do think that way. I wonder sometimes if I don't *look* for trouble, unconsciously, because it's got my name on it, if you know what I mean."

"I know what you mean. Whether the reason is valid may be irrelevant."

He inspected her face. "But how can you decide whether what's making you anxious isn't something to be anxious about? Or whether you're seeing a problem that isn't there?"

"Yes, that's the trouble. Knowing what's real." She bent and kissed his bare shoulder.

"Things are so precarious? That's how you see it?"

"I suppose so. I'm a worrier."

Friday morning Rita said, "Larry, I'm feeling guilty. It's been two days since we've been to the conference. We've barely left the room. Enough's enough, my scientific satyr. I'm going downstairs and put in an appearance. This is the last day, remember?"

"So it is."

"What about you?"

"I'll lie here and not think of you even once. Rita," he called as she started to dress, "when you get back to California, what are your plans?"

"Plans?"

"I was thinking. You're on a sabbatical. It doesn't matter where you take it. What's wrong with Washington? The research facilities are terrific. You could get acquainted with government operations intimately."

"Intimately?"

"I work for the government."

She looked at him from the mirror. "Are you asking me to live with you?"

"That's what I meant."

"I'll give it serious consideration," she said airily, and left.

He lay on his back, smiling, immersed in the blank expanse of ceiling. It seemed to him that she had accepted, in a bantering way. So that was how things happened when they were right between a man and a woman. Easily. No drama. Just a few words. You could spend years fussing about, and bang! There it was, just like that.

The phone rang. "Larry? Hal Anderson. How's the weather down there?" the voice said cheerfully.

Too cheerfully. Pick went tense. "Warm," he said. "In fact, it's hot."

"Aren't you lucky! It's freezing up here."

"I'm not partial to warm weather," Pick replied, longing to small-talk forever. "I can't take the heat. Gives me a rash. I'd rather be on the ski slopes."

"Not today you wouldn't. I had the same idea and I checked the snow conditions. There isn't any snow. Just cold," Anderson said rapidly. "Is it safe to talk on an open line?"

"I think so. Nobody would be listening here."

"Nor here." After a hiatus Anderson spoke again. This time his speech was slower, his voice subdued. "Larry, I'm worried. I modeled out the figures six ways from Sunday. Computer models are only abstractions. The instrument can tell you what the climate might be like if you moved the Rocky Mountains to the East Coast, which doesn't mean you will. The model's just a research tool."

That's how a doctor would sound if he were about to tell you the biopsy showed cancer, Pick thought. "Go on."

"Based on the numbers you gave me, as the computer projects them, there is reason to fear that world climate may change, may already be changing, in a sense."

"How far off is it?" Pick asked quickly.

"How far off is what?"

"The climate change. Centuries?"

"I don't believe you heard me. I said that the change might already be in its opening stages."

The engineer hadn't heard because he hadn't wanted to. He whispered, "Already?"

"According to the models, if you want to believe them. That doesn't mean the big heat is just around the corner—I can't get a reading on when that'll start. But other things could happen earlier."

"Like what?"

"Like highly variable and violent weather."

"Which is what the weather's been like lately."

"Yes. But remember all this is surmise. You'd need much harder evidence to prove anything."

"Or convince anybody. All right, Hal, thanks. I'll be in touch next week from Washington. Not a word to anyone, remember."

Pick reclined on the pillow, suddenly exhausted. What was he supposed to do? Few would give credence if he talked, but neglect would be anything but benign.

"There's a hurricane watch in effect," Rita told him when she entered the room. "Not that you'd know anything about it.

77

You've probably forgotten the outside *exists*, you've been in the room so long. Get dressed. I can't bear the sight of your hairy self any longer." She laughed and lit a cigarette.

"When is the hurricane supposed to strike?"

"Sunday. Maybe sooner."

"Jesus," he said fretfully, "a hurricane this late in the year." *Variable and violent weather.*

She was saying, "It probably won't amount to anything if it comes at all, but I guess I ought to get out of here in a hurry in case the planes stop flying."

He sat up. "I thought we might stay on a few days, Rita. It might be the last chance I'll have for a vacation for a while. Things may get pretty hectic."

"I have to be in California on Monday. I have things to attend to."

"Can't they wait a little?"

"I wish they could but they can't."

The talk with Anderson had made him feel melancholy, and wanting her with him, he sounded more demanding than he meant. "Come on, what are a few days?"

"I have a schedule."

He insisted, "Where your work's concerned, it seems like a couple of days wouldn't make a difference."

"My work doesn't matter as far as *you're* concerned. You don't think much of sociology, do you? Probably not much of women, either. You think your work is more important than mine?"

"Mine is more immediate, that's all," he said, raising his voice.

"And earthshaking!"

"Let's don't fight. Didn't I ask you to live with me?"

"What about my career?"

"Bring it with you. What's wrong with Washington?"

"What's wrong with California? You come there, big shot."

"Rita, I run an organization. I can't take it with me."

"I *knew* I shouldn't have started with you so fast. You don't know the first thing about me. People work for me too! I have a research operation. Projects, grants . . ."

He knew he was acting crankily but he couldn't help himself. "Jesus, you're a drudge."

"Like you, huh? But I'm not a drudge! You're older. You're established. I'm just starting to make my way and you ask me to give it all up."

"I didn't ask you to give up anything! I just suggested new scenery. I wanted to have you close to me, or did, before I saw that work is all you care about. That is, if it's really work that drags you back to the coast."

"I could find a lot of reasons for returning," she said coldly.

"So that's how you feel."

"That's how I feel."

"To hell with you."

"To hell with you!"

8
CHAPTER

"Don't answer it," Doris muttered urgently.

"Have to." Finley picked it up, knowing who the call was from. "Hello. Just a second."

"Must you?"

"Forgive me, baby." He breathed strongly for a few moments, and then, on his side, returned to the telephone. "Yes, George. . . . Very funny. . . . OK, I'll be right over." He put the receiver down and repeated, with a quick caress, "Sorry."

"Me too, Frank."

"In the morning, hon. Sooner if we're lucky."

"Jesus. Saturday night."

"What does it matter what night it is?" Finley switched on the bed lamp, rose from the bed and began to look for his jockey shorts. He was a medium-sized man in his late thirties, with a trim physique, close-cropped blond hair and thin lines around his eyes. He shivered a little in the cold from the air-conditioner as he put on khaki pants, loafers and a sports shirt.

"You could have waited fifteen minutes," Doris said reproachfully.

He stared at the long tan body she was covering with the sheet and a light blanket. "You make it sound like I want to go."

"Fifteen minutes isn't much."

"My head would have been elsewhere," he told her truthfully.

It was already. For twelve long days the Center had been tracking the indecisive fury as it wandered leisurely from its birthplace off the African coast to its present position north of Hispaniola. The storm couldn't decide whether to grow up or merely fade back into the great humid womb from which it came. Finley's hope had been that the depression would lose force, but George Dalton had reported that "it" was changing. A change that merited a midnight telephone call could only be for the worse.

As he drove from Key Biscayne to the University of Miami, where the National Hurricane Center was housed, Finley realized that the depression worried him. There was something persistent about it, like a threat that would finally come true. Keeping in touch with the Center by phone in his capacity as director, he had been touring eastern coastal areas as far north as Georgia to talk about hurricanes and apathy. In recent years the hurricanes had been generally moving into the Gulf of Mexico and avoiding the East; the few hurricanes that hit the East had caused little damage. The people there had either forgotten or didn't know in the first place what a terrifying event a killer storm could be. Floridians lacked a disaster sense, like most Americans. In their optimism, belief in their own power and superiority and their preoccupation with success and instant sensory gratification, they refused to concede that nature could be dangerous.

As he left the air-conditioned car, Finley felt the heat again, heavy heat, oppressive and unprecedented for this late in the year. It felt almost like summer. A speculation brushed Finley's mind but he chased it away as too improbable. Automatically he glanced at the fifth-story windows, ablaze with light. The Center had a double role, as hurricane harbinger and lead forecast station for the state, and a full staff worked there round the clock. Upstairs, the office resonated with the sounds of people and machines. At the teletype Finley saw that the latest notice had just gone out putting the storm's rotary wind speed at 50 mph. Thirty-nine mph was the dividing line between a depression and a tropical storm.

Finley looked around for George Dalton, the duty meteorologist. A short, energetic, ruddy-faced man, Dalton held the latest photo from SMS 1, a geostationary weather satellite in fixed orbit over the equator. The SMS, keeping its silent watch over a quarter of the globe, had been tracking the disturbance since its inception; every half hour, in an electronic spasm, it communicated the results to earth. At Finley's approach, Dalton looked up and said, "Evening, Frank. Sorry to have rousted you from bed."

The other grunted at the formality. Since Finley, as the director, was ultimately responsible for issuing hurricane warnings, Dalton had no choice but to summon him, whether Finley liked it or not. Finley asked, "Well, do we have a hurricane on our hands?"

Over the years, meteorologists had learned to interpret storm characteristics from the photos, including the speeds of interior winds, though not perfectly. Dalton talked briefly and arcanely about closed isobars and rotary circulation aloft. "The prognosticator believes it'll curve back to sea. It sure hasn't so far."

Finley studied the photo, a blowup of part of the satellite

picture. It showed, in whorls and misty contours, the configuration of the storm. If Finley so decided, a hurricane watch would commence, and, as part of the procedure, the storm would be provided with a female name from lists prepared years in advance by the Weather Service. But he took no action yet, fearing a false alarm. A good many hurricane watches that summer and fall had ended in nothing, and if they miscalled this one too, confidence in the warnings would further diminish. He did, however, send out an advisory.

Finley hung around all night. Photo after photo revealed a gradual but steady rise in wind velocity as the storm fed on the hot sea like a baby on a nipple. As it grew, its appetite increased also, to sustain itself and grow further, and always there was the sea with heat in an endless supply. Finley's apprehension increased with the storm, until finally, just after 7 A.M., the telephone rang once more. The weather station at Nassau reported that tides had begun to overflow the beaches. Finley looked at Dalton, who was calculating the wind speeds again. "We're getting close," Dalton said.

"OK, that's it," said Finley.

Reflecting the change in the storm's status, the men moved quickly to a large room, colored red, known as "Hurricane Central." Two thin strips of plastic tape marched across a map that took up one entire wall. The strips were yellow at first, for warning, changing to red for hurricane. Both passed through the Caribbean, below the Keys, and into the Gulf. The strips represented Angie and Barbara, the only two hurricanes of the year so far. Dalton placed the beginning of another yellow strip on the map, then went to a red telephone with hot lines and began to make calls.

In the old days, a man in Finley's position would long since have dispatched a reconnaissance aircraft to penetrate the wall and measure the wind speed about the eye, the important index of hurricane strength, but with the coming of satellites, planes were used only when the outlook seemed critical.

Finley ordered a recon aircraft from Keesler Air Force Base at Biloxi, Mississippi. A hurricane watch had begun. If the storm's interior wind speeds reached 74 mph, she would be officially a hurricane.

The plane, a slow-moving Lockheed-Hercules turbojet, wouldn't reach the storm for three hours and Frank Finley went home for a while. Doris and the children were still asleep, and he lay down beside her. He dreamed: Low against the horizon a long black banner swept across the sky toward Miami.

It was after eleven when Finley returned to the Center. He went straight to Hurricane Central.

Finley assumed that the Lockheed-Hercules would be ready to rendezvous with the storm, but the craft, he learned, had turned back with engine trouble. Only one other plane had been available and a crew hastily assembled. The second plane was airborne and would reach the storm at noon.

In Hurricane Central, Finley found a tall thin man named Grimes who had replaced Dalton as duty meteorologist. He sat at a curved red desk, with lighted screens on the red wall before him. On one screen flashed profiles of previous storms that had resembled this one in location, size and intensity. The other showed, in swirling sequence, a composite of the satellite photos—the storm's development during the past twenty-four hours. "You're just in time, Dr. Hurricane," Grimes told him. "According to our numbers this is now a full-fledged hurricane and she's getting bigger by the hour. This storm could be real mean."

"Prog?" asked Finley.

"Still south of Key West."

"Interior wind speeds?"

"Close to one hundred in the eye wall, and building fast."

"Lord. How do you do, Cindy."

Winds of that size put Cindy on the Scale 2 bracket. Finley considered placing an emergency call to the Governor of Florida, but decided to wait. The point of such a call would be to put evacuation procedures in readiness but there was no real indication that Cindy would hit Florida, and in any case her drift over the ocean was slow.

Instead, Finley composed another advisory. Then he modeled Cindy's future performance based on information from ships, coastal radar, island weather stations and satellite data, which he processed into the Center's computer, in turn tied into a much larger one at the National Meteorological Center at Camp Springs, Maryland. He learned that Cindy's interior wind speeds might reach 150 mph or higher—a Scale 5 hurricane, the worst.

"God!" Finley exclaimed. He grabbed the satellite photo again. From her portrait Cindy appeared as a flat white spiral that drifted along the sea surface, a minor, almost tranquil, eddy in the immense chalice of atmosphere. She looked incapable of causing harm. He glanced at the wall clock. 12:15. *"Where* is that goddam plane?" he asked nobody in particular.

The red phone in Hurricane Central chose that moment to ring, and Grimes grabbed it. "The recon plane," he muttered to Finley and began to scribble the numbers provided by the airborne meteorologist. Quickly translated, these figures gave precise information about the storm from the plane's radar and other instruments. Cindy had an eye no more than 5 miles in diameter, and eye walls 20 miles thick. The storm system measured no more than 300 miles across. Contrary to popular conception, the most deadly hurricanes were compact storms with tiny eyes around which the wind whirled with maximum intensity. Cindy was a dense mass of the greatest energy the planet could generate.

As the plane circled the wall, searching for a weak spot through which to enter the eye, Finley discovered a hangnail but resisted the urge to bite it. He had flown in a weather recon plane in the Air Force—like many meteorologists he had been trained by the military—and sometimes missed the action. He knew how it felt when the plane lurched wildly, wings flapping, fuselage groaning. An aircraft could plummet 1,000 feet in a downdraft, rise as though lifted by an invisible cord. Only one recon plane had been lost in the history of the Weather Service, but still . . . Suddenly the meteorologist aboard the plane began to talk again, and Finley said quietly, "Put it on the speaker."

Static crackled. "OK," the voice shouted, "it looks like we've found a hole. We're going in. Holy horseshit, we're descending. We've got Buck Rogers for a pilot. He wants to try it low. Told him Air Force regs put the basement at two thousand feet, but we're lower than that. Son of a bitch. . . ."

Clutching another satellite transmission, Dalton rushed back into the room yelling, "Listen, we're way off. Cindy's developed tremendous winds in the wall in the last half hour."

"Tell them to go up. Tell them to leave," Finley barked at Grimes.

Grimes talked aimlessly into the mouthpiece. "I can't get through any longer," he shouted.

The voice from the plane arrived in a shroud of static. "You guys are nuts. Wind speed in here is 155 mph. Central pressure 27.9. We're almost in the eye now. I hope we can get out. I hope . . ."

Finley now knew that Cindy was a Scale 5 hurricane, just as the computer predicted. He also suspected from the photo

86

Dalton handed him that Cindy had begun to change course. It was now 12:20. He called Doris and told her to get ready to leave.

At 12:27, the voice said from the plane, "We made it."

The storm was gaining speed and boiled across the ocean at 15 mph. If she maintained present course and speed she would reach the city as early as 9 P.M.

Warnings poured from the Center on TV and radio. Finley finally reached the Governor at a football game between the Miami Dolphins and the Baltimore Colts at the Orange Bowl.

"Governor Hollis speaking," said the politician's modulated voice.

"Frank Finley, Director of the Hurricane Center here. Sir, we've got a problem. It looks more and more like Cindy is heading our way, and will strike this evening. Governor, this is a serious storm."

"Well, what are you asking me to do, Finley?"

"Start the procedures for forcible evacuation in case it's needed. I think it will be."

"Are you sure it'll hit? It looks fine here."

Finley felt impatient. He sometimes wished society were organized like the military, with a clear chain of command.

He explained, "Don't let that fool you. Weather is deceptive. Anyway, nothing is certain in this business. It's like politics," Finley offered with a short, sarcastic laugh. He hated politicians in general and, at this moment, Governor Hollis in particular. "We can't be too careful. I'd like to suggest . . ." He hesitated, knowing what the reaction would be, but at least he had gone on record. ". . . that the football game be called off. It takes time to relocate people. Traffic . . ."

"Stop the game? What are you talking about?" Hollis cried. "If I stop it—and I'm not certain I have the right—and the

87

storm doesn't come here, what'll I look like, I ask you? Like a panicky old woman. What do you mean by 'this evening'?"

"Nine o'clock, maybe."

"All right, the game will be over at four. That's five full hours."

"More like three. Things will be happening by then, if not before. We could get wind bursts later this afternoon, in fact, and high tides."

"OK, three hours," the Governor said. "It's still enough time to get people out. Let's wait."

"OK." Finley wished he were back in the Air Force.

"I'll call you later to see how it looks. If it's as bad as you say, I'll declare an emergency," the Governor said.

". . . destructive winds and high tides to strike south Florida tonight. The Weather Service advises that a hurricane emergency warning has been issued for both sides of the Florida peninsula from Stuart and Venice southward and the Keys southward as far as Tavernier. Safety precautions should be rushed with all possible urgency on the southeast coast and completed by no later than six P.M."

The football game was canceled in the third quarter.

At the Hurricane Center much later on, Finley could barely believe what the instruments told him. Hurricane Cindy had hit Miami with winds of over 200 miles an hour, exceeding the notorious storm that ravaged Mississippi in 1970—a record. Low-lying areas like Key Biscayne were covered with water, and dozens of houses had collapsed—he hoped his own hadn't been one of them—as they had in Coral Gables and large sections of downtown Miami, hundreds in all. The big hotels on Miami Beach stood, according to the last calls before the phones went out, but with ground floors gutted completely by the enormous tides. Casualty figures were mounting rapidly.

"Well, I think she's going out to sea. I don't think there's any further danger to the mainland," said Frank Finley to Grimes.

"Thank God. My folks live in Petersburg." He went outside.

Finley rose and took his jacket from a hook. He was seated again when Grimes reentered the room. "You've got a visitor."

"A visitor? It's after two!"

"Says he has to see you. He has credentials. He's the Deputy Director of that CRISES outfit."

"CRISES? The disaster boys? Well, he's come to the right place. Send him in, will you?"

Grimes returned followed by a tall, strongly built man with a dark, intense face. "Dr. Finley? I'm Lawrence Pick."

"Pleased to meet you. Won't you sit down? Pardon me for not standing. I'm too bushed."

"I'm sure you are," Pick said in a deep voice as he sat by Finley's desk, seeming to engulf the small metal chair. "Do you have the casualty figures?"

"Incomplete ones. It was terrible. Almost four hundred so far."

"Jesus." The man was silent for a moment, then said, "I wouldn't have bothered you, except I have to leave early tomorrow, if the planes are flying."

"They'll be flying," Finley assured him. "The hurricane's over. What's on your mind, Dr. Pick?"

"I, uh . . ." Pick glanced meaningfully toward Grimes, who stood nearby, his face a mass of curiosity.

Finley said softly, "Don, would you run another check on Cindy's course? I'd just like to be certain."

"Sure," Grimes said with a frown and departed.

Pick said in a low voice, "Dr. Finley, does this hurricane strike you as a strange storm?"

Finley hesitated. He wasn't one to engage in speculation, but the big man's serious face encouraged him. "Yes, as a matter of fact, it does. I thought about it all evening, when I had time. I mean, Cindy shillied around like she didn't know where she was headed, or as if contradictory forces were operating on her. Then she built up as rapidly as any hurricane I can remember and her wind speeds were just enormous. It's one for the books, even without considering how late in the season it is. Finally she hit the Florida mainland, which represents a change from normal hurricane patterns in recent years . . ." He faltered.

Pick said thoughtfully, sounding tired and perhaps depressed, "Could Cindy have been related to abnormally high temperature in the tropics?"

"I wondered about that too. Hurricanes act like ventilators to let excess heat out of the tropics, and it might follow that there's more heat down there than there ought to be. I believe something funny is going on. I'm trying to figure out what."

Pick said suddenly, "Dr. Finley, if we need you in Washington this week, could you make it?"

"Sure, I guess so," Finley replied, surprised.

Pick lay awake in his downtown hotel room, staring at the dark through the window. He felt like a solitary sentinel guarding a sleeping army against a silent, ineffable, ominous, deadly presence. The hurricane, he believed, had been a signal.

9
CHAPTER

BEFORE HE LEFT FLORIDA, Pick made two telephone calls. One started an emergency clearance on Rita Havu. The security people objected to having to work so fast, but Pick prevailed. The other, to Edmunston's secretary, was about the boss's schedule, which turned out to be tight for the day. The engineer preempted an appointment with a demographer—the overpopulation question could wait.

That afternoon, as they sat down on either side of the old man's polished desk, Edmunston remarked, "I told you to have a rest, and what do you do but find a hurricane. Only you, Larry."

"Not much to joke about, Rufus. An awful lot of people died."

Edmunston's face changed swiftly. "Yes, Cindy was a lousy storm. Too bad."

"Most of them died because they didn't want to heed the warnings. Jesus, what does it take to make them listen?"

"The imprecision of the forecasts is the problem."

"One of them," the engineer said brusquely. "Another is that the goddam fools believe they lead charmed lives. Either something won't happen at all or it'll strike elsewhere. I worry that if serious trouble came, Americans wouldn't be able to handle it, because of that attitude."

"You worry about everything," Edmunston replied with a snort. "But how come you didn't get out of Miami yourself before the storm?"

"There was somebody I wanted to talk to," Pick said. "Look, Rufus, this heat thing—we've got to take it seriously, I'm afraid."

The Director sighed deeply. "Is there something new?"

"Yes. I had computer weather models made. They showed that a climate change might be underway. They also indicated . . ."

" 'Might' . . . 'indicated,' " Edmunston protested.

". . . that the first symptom of the change might be violent weather. Like Cindy. There's a leading hurricane expert in Miami named Finley, who's with the Weather Service. He thinks Cindy might have been the direct result of a tropical heat pocket such as a localized CO_2 jump would cause."

"Would you bet your professional reputation on it?" the old man asked with a shrewd look.

Pick sat silently for a moment. "Of course I wouldn't, no."

"It's just like you—to make a possibility, and a slim one in my view, into a probability, even a certainty," Edmunston said.

The engineer jammed his back into the chair. "What do we do, Rufus—wait? Probably nothing will happen, but then again it might be too late to do anything at all. What's proof? Maybe the hurricane is far from conclusive. . . . I know, I know, you could assemble a dozen experts to say there's no relationship, but what if one exists? I think we have to act *as if* there's going to be a global heat increase at some point, and if we're wrong we're wrong."

Edmunston rose and went to the window, thin shoulders

stooped. He sounded almost hurt. "I'm trying to do my job, Larry, just like you're trying to do yours. We have a conflict of interest here. I want to protect the integrity of this outfit so it can go on performing useful work. I can't permit the Service to risk its standing with a prophecy that can't be proved, that most people won't believe in and which most likely won't be fulfilled anyway. I don't think you've examined the political aspects of this as the White House would see it. They're horrendous." He turned abruptly to face the younger man. "Let's compromise. Let's put it out as a speculation paper. We'll have done our duty and at the same time have been relieved of a responsibility I frankly don't want."

"No!" Pick's fist hit wood. "It won't work."

"Take it easy," the Director warned.

The big man's voice turned pleading. "Look, it wouldn't get the right results. Either they'd take it only as one more speculation or the press might play it up. It would become an issue right away. The politicians would grab it and take sides. The public would become so confused that it wouldn't know what to think. People would turn their backs on the whole business. Even if we tried to limit the information to scientists only, someone is sure to get in front of the TV cameras and blab. You know how scientists are. I'd like to go to the National Academy or WMO* with this but I really think it's better to put together the proof first. No, before we say a word, we ought to have the whole thing laid out, with possible countermeasures to recommend. We need a plan. Until we have one, only those directly involved in the project should be told what the real situation is. The risk of premature release is too great."

Edmunston cried, "Project? What project?"

"I want to assemble a team of experts."

---

* World Meteorological Organization

"What experts?"

"I have them in mind. Murray Baxter, of course. I told you about Frank Finley. He runs the Hurricane Warning Center at Miami. Kline, the chemist whose paper we discussed. A climate modeler named Hal Anderson who did the computer study on this for me. All seem first-rate, as good as anybody we can get. I'd like to bring them to Washington this week."

"This week! You *are* in a hurry. It would be so much better to wait until there's just a little more proof. I've talked to the Science Adviser, who's skeptical, to say the least."

"The hell with him."

Edmunston flushed slightly. "Is that your complete roster?"

Pick answered, "No. I'd like a disaster sociologist. I checked on Paul Warburg, who consults for us, but he's out of the country, and to bring him back would look too damn suspicious. There aren't many good ones. I've settled on a person named Havu whose paper on earthquake prediction we talked about."

"I remember. You liked his work."

"I met *her* in Florida," Pick confessed.

Edmunston sat down and stared at his Deputy bleakly, in the manner of a boss who was trapped into action by a relentless subordinate. Shaking his long white hair, he muttered finally, "All right, go ahead, in secret. But I want to know what ILLIAC's got on these people—we can't tolerate screwballs running loose in the hole, which is where you intend to work, I suppose."

Pick nodded.

"Is that all then?" Edmunston's hand began to reach toward the switch that deactivated the electronic screen.

Pick said abruptly, "No. I want to launch a weather probe using military facilities to ensure security. We have the right to do that through the ARPA contract."

"All right. All right. You understand, don't you, that this might be the end of you?"

Pick said, "Yes, I know."

A section of the National Scientific Emergency Act provided that the FBI should assemble dossiers on all physical scientists in the country, in case they had to be mobilized. This part of the Act had been declared unconstitutional by the Supreme Court on the grounds that it invaded privacy, and the files were supposed to have been destroyed, but the information had been secretly retained in a computer at the Department of Justice, where ILLIAC had come upon it on one of its routine probes of other computers conducted in the middle of the night.

Pick had never bothered to look at the information ILLIAC VII possessed, but since a check was to be run on the prospective team, he retrieved the file on himself first, thinking that if he were represented accurately the others would be also.

That evening at Fort Davis he asked ILLIAC for the codes of the names in question. His own turned out to be PLM—39—E—E. He figured: initials, last name first; year of birth; field (engineering); geographical area in which lives (East). He pressed buttons:

user: biopers PLM—39—E—E
audio:
The female voice said promptly:
PICK, LAWRENCE MARSHALL. ENGINEER. BORN, SONESTOWN, PENNSYLVANIA, 1939. EDUCATION . . .

The biographical information left out nothing of consequence, and included his childless marriage and divorce. Then followed a personality appraisal—the "pers" of "biopers," for Biographical-Personality Index. The voice chanted:

95

SUBJECT HIGHLY REGARDED BY COLLEAGUES FOR INTELLI-
GENCE, LEADERSHIP, ORIGINALITY, PURPOSE, DRIVE. LOY-
ALTY UNQUESTIONED. BUT NEGATIVE FEEDBACK HAS BEEN
RECEIVED. SUBJECT IS ACCUSED OF BEING AN ALARMIST.
OTHER DESCRIPTIVE TERMS THAT HAVE BEEN USED ARE:
PESSIMISTIC, GLOOMY, ANXIOUS. HIS PERSONALITY MAY, IN
SHORT, CONTRIBUTE TO HIS SENSE OF A WORLD IN PERIL.
SUBJECT MIGHT EXAGGERATE THE POSSIBILITY OF CATAS-
TROPHE. HIS ASSESSMENTS MUST SOMETIMES BE VIEWED
WITH SKEPTICISM.

Son of a bitch! Pick thought angrily. Whoever had com-
piled the dossier had talked to Edmunston.

He knew, he thought, all the pertinent facts about Baxter
and ordered the biopers on Bertram Kline next. Kline had
come to NCAR from the Scripps Oceanographic Institute at La
Jolla. In his mid-forties, he was rated tops as a chemist. He had
grown children from his first marriage but none by his second
to a woman some years his junior. When a student, Kline had
been a member of the Young People's Socialist League, but
there was no reason to doubt his loyalty. He was described as
careful, cautious, meticulous. Then came an item that jarred
the engineer. A dozen years before, Kline had been hospitalized for mental illness—annoyingly, the dossier failed to be
more specific than that—and Pick was forced to wonder
whether to recruit the man. He decided in the affirmative. The
hospitalization had been brief, there had been no recurrence,
and a dozen years was a long time. Besides, checking dates,
Pick saw that Kline's trouble coincided with the breakup of his
first marriage, and the engineer remembered his emotional
state when his own marriage ended. He had been depressed
enough to consult a psychiatrist.

At thirty-eight, Frank Finley had been a meteorologist in the

Air Force during the Vietnam war, afterward obtained his Ph.D. and joined the Weather Service, where he continued to study and model hurricanes until he became one of the leading authorities in the world. He lived with his wife and two children in Miami. The biopers described him as steady, cheerful, open, friendly, calm—perfect, thought Pick. Except . . . Finley had the slightest heart anomaly—not enough to keep him out of the Air Force but enough to prevent him from being a pilot. Well, if he was fit for military service, he could handle the work in the hole.

Harold Anderson was thought to have a brilliant future in his specialty, climate modeling. He had a B.A. in math from the University of Oregon and a Ph.D. in climatology from Princeton, where he lived with a young wife and an infant. Anderson was said to be highly intelligent. He was described as ambitious, and he worked only on projects which might advance his scientific career.

The file only indexed "hard" or physical scientists, not "soft" or social ones, and therefore lacked information on Rita Havu.

The next day, Tuesday, Edmunston, in his prestigious role as Director of CRISES, telephoned the four recruits with the same message: urgently requested to come to Washington on Thursday; airline tickets, ground transportation, accommodations, all expenses provided, daily consultant fee of $145. Short job leaves had been arranged. . . . But the old man would explain nothing more. Curious and flattered, the men accepted at once, but not Rita Havu. The woman insisted she had too much to do.

"We'll see about that," Pick muttered.

An automated buoy, jerked this way and that by the waves, sent signals by radio to a satellite that beamed them to Navy

Fleet Weather. The helicopter had a long thin snout attached to its nose, like the beak of a bird. It flew low over the ocean with the snout barely skimming the surface, as though the bird drank.

"What's this for?" a crewman asked the pilot through his headset.

"God knows," said the pilot. "For science, whatever that means."

The nuclear sub rose from the bottom, sucking in water at various levels as she went. The sub took the temperature of the sea.

Above, Air Force bombers coursed the skies, leaving silvery contrails. The jets traveled with intake valves open so that air passed over delicate instruments in a continuous rush. On control panels dials turned, needles jiggled.

Balloons went far higher than the reaches of the planes. Sensors radioed reports to ships and ground stations.

From the ocean depths to the top of the sky the world was being searched for clues.

On Thursday, December 1, at different times of day, Finley, Kline and Anderson arrived in Washington and reported to Pick at the gray Georgian building on Connecticut Avenue. All had been previously cleared for service under the National Scientific Emergency Act. They were instructed individually by Pick on the need for total security. The engineer said, "OK. A room's been reserved for you at the Hay-Adams. In the morning, at eight sharp, go to the street with your bag. Don't worry about checking out of the hotel. You'll find a green minibus with Maryland license plates parked there. Board it. There will be two other passengers. Please don't engage in speculations of any kind, and not a word to your family or associates. Sorry about the cloak-and-dagger stuff, but that's how it has to be."

The minibus waited at the curb, doors open, motor idling, and at 8 A.M. sharp, Finley arrived with an overnight bag, closely followed by a stocky man with a round face who introduced himself as Harold Anderson. They waited in silence and finally an older man with thinning brown hair, narrow cheeks and pouches beneath his eyes climbed slowly into the bus. "Sorry," Bertram Kline said. "I overslept. Tired, I guess."

They started off. The bus had curtains on the windows and an opaque screen behind the front seat that blocked a view of the road. Nobody spoke. There was nothing to do, see or say.

PART III
THE HOLE

10
CHAPTER

THE EFFECT OF THE CONFERENCE ROOM, where one wall, entirely of glass, looked out on the turning globe, was not unlike being in a spaceship high above the earth. The room contained a computer terminal on a slender metal stalk, a large screen, a whiteboard and a large conference table, round, to eliminate the suggestion of rank. In scientific endeavor, all men were equal, in theory at least.

The calendar clock on the wall silently snapped out the minutes, seconds and tenths of seconds.

DEC. 2 FRI AM 9 02 42 7 . . . 8 . . . 9 . . .
DEC. 2 FRI AM 9 02 43 1 . . . 2 . . . 3 . . .

Pick tapped the polished tabletop with a pencil. He thought: *Time will be a real problem.* We've got to hurry. If anything's happening, it'll have to be dealt with right away, before it reaches a critical point. He experienced a strong sense of futility, as though the future were running backward, toward him, and, when it intersected with the advancing present, it would cease to exist. But the future couldn't cease to exist unless at some point the present was destroyed with it. *Jesus Christ, stop,* he told himself.

DEC. 2 FRI AM 9 17 21 5 . . . 6 . . . 7 . . .

He found himself asking if he had made a mistake to push things this far. The big computer at Sverdlovsk, a Siberian city where Soviet weather modifications had been headquartered before the treaty, and which still served as the Russians' climate intelligence center, had been queried the night before by means of a spy satellite masked as a meteorological one. Electronic bursts activated the Soviet machine, which, in seconds, and with no outward manifestation, was made to pour forth a mass of information that in turn was retransmitted when the American satellite passed over the United States. Digesting the information, ILLIAC found no indication that the Sovs were running unusual tests. They suspected nothing about a potential climate change then, which made Pick feel lonelier than ever. The meteorological probe had failed to produce anything of significance, though fresh data still poured in. Maybe all this effort would be pointless because there was no problem in the first place. That would be a great relief to Lawrence Pick, and yet, somehow, you didn't get medals for being wrong. . . .

There was still time to quit. A cursory runthrough with the incoming experts. Conclusion: Not enough to go on, but we'll keep an eye out. Send the men home. Edmunston would be delighted. Chance to make up with Rita. Start a life with her. A normal existence for a change.

Why not? Let somebody else worry about it. Sooner or later . . .

Stop!

DEC. 2 FRI AM 9 20 17 5 . . . 6 . . . 7 . . .

"Visitors! Visitors, Dr. Pick!" said a strident voice over the announcement system.

A few more minutes passed. Pick sat staring at the turning globe through the glass wall. Then the doors slid open and three men entered single file, each uniformed in white. Surprise streaked their faces at their first glimpse of the hole.

Anderson's bantering tone was unable to conceal a note of wonder. "Unbelievable. Is this where God lives?"

"Impressive, all right," Finley observed.

Kline, the chemist, said in a dry voice, "I never imagined anything like this existed."

"It doesn't exist. Please don't forget that," Pick cautioned them.

"Could you tell us what it's all for?" Finley asked.

Pick was evasive. "Not entirely, no. It has a number of functions but primarily the facility monitors and simulates environmental conditions throughout the world. We want to be able to predict and, hopefully, prevent and control trouble in the biosphere." The engineer explained the work of the men on the tiers but failed to mention weather warfare surveillance or ILLIAC's spying on other computers.

"But why the secrecy?" Kline asked softly. "You practically made me swear an oath."

"Well, in the event a place were needed for intense research if a crisis arose, you might want total privacy," Pick answered.

"Has it ever been used for that purpose?" Anderson asked.

"Not before this." He glanced at the clock. "Let's begin. A woman is coming from California to join us but her plane must be late. Edmunston's picking her up." He chuckled a little. "She's not likely to be in a very good mood. Well, none of you have the full picture of what we're about to do, so let me sketch it in a preliminary way. . . ."

The sharp intercom voice said, "Dr. Edmunston's arrived with a visitor."

"Send them down," Pick said into the air. "Skip the uniforms this once. And I want the conference room sealed, please. Oh, have Murray Baxter come in now."

"Yes, sir."

They sat in silence until Anderson asked, "What's the reason for the uniforms?"

"The hole contains some extremely delicate equipment. Even street dirt might affect it. But since we'll stay in the conference room for now, it doesn't matter."

Baxter entered, was introduced and took a seat. Then the doors opened and the Director arrived with a woman at his side, taller than he. Having glanced sharply at Pick, Rita Havu's only visible reaction to the panorama before her was an almost imperceptible widening of her eyes, which turned next to the five men seated at the round table like the points of a star. Edmunston was saying, "Dr. Rita Havu, Drs. Kline, Baxter, Finley, Anderson. And Dr. Lawrence Pick, whom I believe you've met." Edmunston grinned.

"Hello, Dr. Havu," Pick said. She nodded coldly.

The newcomers sat down. Edmunston leaned forward, saying in a serious tone, "Larry Pick will chair the meeting, since we're in his ballpark, but I have several observations. The first is that we are dealing with a very unusual kind of situation, one of potentially enormous magnitude in terms of international security, and yet of a very low probability order, so low that without Larry Pick's extremely energetic insistence you would not be here at all. Very well, you are here. I hope, in fact, I am confident, that your function will be to disprove the theory of an impending heat rise . . ."

"Heat rise?" Kline murmured with a frown.

"Larry will brief you on that, Dr. Kline. What I am getting to is this: In the gray, little-understood area in which you will work, there will be more room for assumptions—I mean guesswork—than is normal in science. I humbly suggest that you do not exercise your imaginations, but stick with that which can be demonstrated beyond reasonable doubt. We ask an explosive question, and to reach answers that are both pessimistic *and* wrong could have more serious consequences than any of you are likely to understand at this juncture. Further, I want to reiterate what all of you have been told—that secrecy is utterly imperative. Not a word of what the problem is must reach *anyone* outside of this circle. All right. My only function is to act as your liaison with the powers that be, should such prove necessary, which I pray it won't." The almost imperceptible hum of the air-conditioner was the only sound in the room. "Larry?"

The engineer had remained impassive during Edmunston's speech. Seeming to shake himself slightly, he said, "Let's review the situation. We'll be working together as volunteers . . ."

"Volunteers?" Rita Havu protested. "Who volunteered? I didn't. My arm was twisted, I'll tell you that. I don't know what you use it for, but you people really have clout."

"I think you'll understand better as we go along, Rita—Dr. Havu," he said, lowering his eyes under the pressure from hers. "Let's hear first from Murray Baxter."

Baxter wiped his steel-rimmed glasses on the sleeve of his white uniform. "A little background might be useful. I'll try to be brief and not technical," he said, mostly for the benefit of the sociologist, though the Director was no whiz at climate either. In the modern conception, Baxter explained, climate was understood as a heat machine, with solar radiation providing the power. Heat controlled winds, tides, rainfall, ice cover and the other elements that comprised the climate system. But heat arriving at the earth's surface had to be disposed of or the world would become intolerably hot. The heat income was balanced by infrared reradiation into space. The basic relation-

107

ship could be expressed by an equation, which Baxter, rising, wrote on the whiteboard with a metal stylus. The result appeared in deep green.

$$Q/A = KeT^4 \quad (4C)$$

Baxter gazed owlishly at the formula and went on, "It means that changes in the heat budget affect surface temperatures." It was commonly believed, he explained, that air pollution, blocking incoming sunlight, was partly responsible for a temperature drop of more than 1° F. in the years between 1940 and 1975, though the cooling had mysteriously stopped since then. A further cooling could lead to a new ice age, and it wouldn't take much, since even small changes in average world temperature were greatly magnified at the poles. Today, industrial pollutants, particles, chemicals and heat entered the atmosphere in ever greater amounts. Such effects were not only local. Climatologically, every place on earth was connected to every other place. Was the ecosystem being overtaxed?

Baxter pressed a button and the formula vanished. In its place he wrote

GREENHOUSE EFFECT

and stood back to study it. If atmospheric CO_2 had begun to jump further, the surface energy budget would be seriously changed. Already CO_2 emission had increased nine times since 1900. The present concentration of atmospheric CO_2 was about 340 parts per million. Some believed it would rise to 400 ppm by the year 2000, which might increase average global temperature by 1.8° F., itself as large a climate change as had occurred in 1,000 years. If CO_2 quantity increased even more, so might global heat. Looking grim, Baxter sat down.

Bertram Kline rubbed the pouches beneath his eyes as though to make them disappear. "That was my fantasy, my awful fantasy. And now you say it might be true."

Finley asked in an easy drawl, "What time frame are we talking about?"

The engineer nodded. "I'd say, publish the facts and let future generations handle it if the heat rise were a couple of centuries off. But it may not be. That's what we're here to find out. The question of when the climate change will occur is basic and we don't know the answer."

"But what's it got to do with me?" the woman cried.

" 'What's it got to do with me?' is exactly what people will ask, and that's what it's got to do with you, Dr. Havu. I'll explain later. Meantime, I estimate we'll be here a week. Nobody expects to hear from you before then—we've already seen to that," Pick replied.

"A week!" the woman said sulkily. "I was told a couple of days!"

"Sorry." He grinned.

He gave them code words that would identify the point at which the world's climate began to change: Condition Green.

The underground facility was completely equipped for a small group. It had simple but amply furnished bedrooms, each with its own lavatory and shower; a small gym with a sauna and sunlamps—the medical officer directed the team to exercise every day; a cafeteria whose so-so food was supplemented by vitamins; a library and rec room with TV.

Inside the head-shaped hill was a maze of laboratories, workshops and programming rooms, all connected by steel-sheathed tubes to the hole where the globe turned. One could easily get lost in such a place, and Rita Havu did on the first afternoon. Pick found her wandering disconsolately down a corridor, poking her head into rooms where white-uniformed technicians toiled. He offered her a tour of the facility. The men got the same later in the day.

109

Rita had been provided with a uniform that, being the only female size available, was much too big for her, and the contours of her lithe figure were lost in the baggy, shapeless gear. There wasn't much to see topside—a view of the countryside and, in the distance, the tips of far-off steeples over leafless trees. She pointed to a swiveling shield. "Is that radar?"

"That," he said in his deep confident voice, "is a . . ."

He didn't finish, and she said, "What does it do?"

"It monitors things."

"What things?"

"I can't tell you. You're not cleared."

There wasn't much to see in the upstairs part of the facility either. Just secretaries, guards, maintenance people, offices. He showed her his. Nothing suggested that he ran the place. Old desk. Old chair. Worn rug. Bare walls. No degrees, certificates, memberships, photos, mementoes. There wasn't a scrap of anything personal, much less sentimental. "How do you know it's *your* office?" she inquired. "You're not much for keepsakes."

"I guess not." His black eyes stared importunately as he bent to kiss her.

She said, "No."

"Am I in deep freeze? What's the matter?"

"You know what's the matter. I dislike you. In fact, I hate you a little. I thought about it all the way to California. Then I put you out of my mind forever, or so I thought."

Pick stepped backward, exclaiming, "But why?"

"Because of the sort of person you are," Rita said excitedly. "You don't give a damn for anybody but yourself. Witness the way you looked at my career! You're insensitive to individuals. I know, I know, you care about the human race. Well, it's easy to like in the abstract, but *what about me?* What was I to you, except an available woman?"

110

"Nonsense, Rita."

"I know a man in California who worships me. That's the kind of man I like—one who respects my accomplishments!"

"But I do respect your accomplishments! Why do you think you're here?"

"Because you want somebody to make love to."

"That isn't it! It's true I wanted you around, but if anyone better qualified had been available I would have snapped him up, believe me."

"Oh, you've done it now. You wanted a *him*. You just couldn't find one, so you settled on me."

"Look, you're misreading. I only meant I was goddam glad that you *were* qualified for a very difficult job."

"Oh yeah? How? What job?"

"Of telling us how to make people accept the inevitable, if it comes to that."

She laughed without humor. "Make *me* accept the inevitable, which is you, in your eyes."

"Rita . . ."

"You'd make a housewife out of me, Larry, I know it, and the last person I wish to be in this world is a housewife. Why do you think I've never married or even lived with anybody? Because I don't want to be controlled."

"Control," he said bitterly. "I thought I was in love with you. Is that control? You're impossible. My bad luck. Let's go below."

To "access," as he called it, the underground part of the facility required a special pass. Armed guards waved them on to big elevators which could only be summoned by an electronic rod that fitted into a slot. Steel doors opened with a startling bang, and they whistled back down six stories until the doors cracked open to reveal the metal tiers and the globe. Pick stepped up to it. "You see here a perfect replica of the

111

planet, on which any conceivable physical occurrence of sufficient magnitude is instantly recorded. See that small square in the mid-Pacific? It's an undersea volcano that's started to erupt. The computer flashes information to the globe automatically. Inside it are thirty-seven thousand miles of electrical wiring," he said with more than a trace of pride.

"Is that so?" answered Havu. She took a cigarette from her pocket and started to light it. His hand moved so rapidly that she felt rather than saw the lighter torn from her hand.

"I'm sorry. You can't smoke here. The plastic covering of the globe is perfect for our purposes but it has one defect. It's extremely combustible." He smiled slightly. "You'd set the world on fire." He pointed to a fire extinguisher that hung from a hook. It seemed strangely old-fashioned in the futuristic setting.

She looked startled. "Who designed all this?"

"I did mostly. It's been in operation less than a year. Some people want to phase it out already. That's the government for you."

He guided her past a door marked COMPWATCH.

"What's in there?"

"I'm not permitted to say."

"And what's that?" She pointed to the door marked CASS.

"Classified 'Top Secret.' Sorry."

"What are those?" She pointed to the tubes which were the laser guns.

"I hope you never have to find out."

The endless sections were all "Top Secret." At last, having gone halfway around the inside of the hollow dome on a metal catwalk, they entered the cafeteria. "I suppose tonight's menu is secret too," she joked over coffee. His smile seemed easier. She went on, "Tell me the truth. Do you really believe this climate thing is as serious as you've presented it?"

112

He stared at her. "Think it's a game?"

"I got the idea from Dr. Edmunston, coming in from the airport, that there might be an error factor of some kind, that there could be no crisis at all . . ."

"Sure, it's possible," he admitted, "though Rufus can be hard to convince about trouble. He likes to look on the bright side."

"What would happen if you're wrong, having undertaken this effort?"

"I'd be sacked," he said bluntly.

"And you're going ahead anyway?"

"Yes."

Strong and handsome as he was, Pick seemed to her lonely and vulnerable at that moment, behind his keen black eyes and the crisp white uniform he wore like armor.

Pick had parceled out the assignments as follows: Kline, the chemist, and Baxter, the meteorologist, were to analyze the data pouring in from the meteorological probes conducted by the military; Finley, the hurricane expert, and Anderson, the climatologist, were to model weather futures based on data already in hand, an enormously complex task that would have been impossible if ILLIAC hadn't already "known" about climate. Pick was to formulate projected levels of energy production and consumption. Havu would explore the shaping of public attitudes.

That so much could have been accomplished by so few was surprising enough; that so many conclusions could have been reached in so short a time was almost unbelievable in retrospect.

On Monday, after a frantic weekend of work, the daily meetings began.

11
CHAPTER

PICK WAITED UNTIL a uniformed aide who served coffee and danish had left the room before he said, "Ready to report, Murray?"

"Not yet."

"Dr. Kline?"

"Not ready," said the dry-voiced chemist.

"Dr. Havu?"

"No."

The engineer shifted. "Drs. Finley and Anderson?"

Finley's easy voice said, "Hal Anderson and I are trying to find out what would happen because of a sharp rise in atmospheric CO_2. It's an immensely difficult problem. The climate system taken as a whole is too complex even for computers— ordinarily, we'd need several computers, but ILLIAC's big enough to work with—so we have to break it down into pieces such as atmosphere, ocean surface layer, deep oceans, wind, albedo—" he glanced at Havu—"the earth's reflectivity, that is. Then there are unknowns, like how big the CO_2 jump is, how much energy will be used in the future, and other questions. We're trying to synthesize all relevant phenomena into a

114

single interacting whole, to learn how the real climate system will operate. So far we've been able to make only one model, which we call 'Earth One.' Hal, you want to run the show?"

"Sure," Anderson said briskly. He turned his round face to a microphone near him on the table and gave instructions. The lights dimmed in the room and the screen glowed.

EARTHWATCH

The word faded and was replaced by other words.

EARTH ONE
YEARS: NOW TO 2100 A.D.
TEMPERATURE CHANGE: INSIGNIFICANT

"What?" Pick asked sharply.

"Our assumption here," Anderson explained, "is that the CO_2 rise continues to be only slightly above normal. In that case it may prove only a temporary phenomenon, or, even if the increase in the rate of increase is permanent, it might not change the climate, especially if the cooling trend proves real. The two effects might cancel each other out. Earth One may be like the present."

"But we don't think so," Finley went on. "More likely, the augmented CO_2 blanket will bring changes." He sipped his coffee and Anderson whispered into the mike. More words appeared.

CLIMATE CHANGE: CLOUDINESS

Finley continued, "This is a positive feedback mechanism—meaning mutual reinforcement. Global heat is about to rise but humidity increases, too, and so does cloud cover, which blocks incoming sunlight, so that temperature remains the same. What you get is a very cloudy world. Agriculture would be seriously affected because you'd have less sunlight. We don't

115

believe that Earth One could support a population of much more than five billion."

"But the projections show six billion by the turn of the century and as high as sixteen billion by 2050," Pick said with a wince.

"People will starve. Lots of them."

"Also, the suicide rate zooms," Havu observed quietly. "Too much cloudiness makes people depressed."

"Well, sunny days will be a rarity but it won't be any warmer. At least, we hope not." Finley permitted himself a rare frown. "There's so much we don't know."

DEC. 6 TUES AM 8 03 21 4 . . . 5 . . . 6 . . .

Murray Baxter opened a file folder filled with handwritten yellow sheets and computer printouts. He explained, "I've been working with atmospheric samples obtained by the Air Force all over the world. I have several observations. One is that the concentration of CO_2 is perceptibly higher in a quadrant of about a thousand square miles in the tropical Atlantic. Let's see it on the globe."

The western hemisphere was facing the window. On it appeared black lines representing latitudes and longitudes, and then, its bottom not far from the equator, a light-green square midway between Africa and South America. Baxter chewed on a temple of his eyeglasses and went on, "That's where the trouble is. The increased concentration lies just above the sea surface, and it's probably causing a heat pocket. The gas has begun to spread slowly, but it's not detected by standard meteorological equipment because it's carried straight up in normal atmospheric upwellings to a height of eighty thousand to one hundred thousand feet. The instrumented balloons give a little confirmation of that. Up there, the gas drifts around. Very occasionally, at dawn or sunset, mostly, it ought to give

116

the sky a greenish tint. There have been a few sightings of that phenomenon. Sooner or later the gas will mix into the global atmosphere."

Pick remembered the greenish Florida sky at dusk. "Then what happens?" he asked.

Baxter shrugged.

"Dr. Kline?"

"Not ready, I'm afraid."

"Dr. Havu?"

"Not yet." She wore a trace of makeup this morning.

"Drs. Finley and Anderson?"

Finley answered, "Yesterday we showed you Earth One. But given the mechanics of this, we don't think it will happen that way. Earth One is just too pat, especially when we factor in assumptions like Murray Baxter's. The violent weather of Earth Two seems more likely. Hal?"

The stocky climatologist was quick to answer. "Regional heat anomalies may cause severe convective storms—we know, for instance, that volcanoes can generate tornadoes. In fact, mesoscale effects would probably be felt long before climatic changes could be documented. That's a big part of the problem. If the climate became unstable, you couldn't prove why.

"You'd get slightly different conditions in the urban regions than elsewhere. The cities are heat islands already because of their intense energy consumption and physical characteristics like paved streets. They're a good deal hotter than the surrounding countryside, especially at night. Downtown Paris is four degrees hotter than its suburbs, and with Manhattan the difference is even greater. You'd get some awfully hot days in the cities—I can imagine an occasional summer day in New York at 110°. A little less in Washington, but more in L.A."

"What are the records for those cities?" Havu interrupted.

"For New York, 107 degrees. For Washington, 102. For

L.A., 108," Anderson answered, without consulting notes. "The American heat record is 134 degrees, in Death Valley, if you want to know, and the world record is 136.4 degrees, in Libya. In places like that it would easily top 150. Let's see the projections." A map flashed on the screen, followed by another. Nobody spoke. "Also, the heat would bring increased rainfall— the cities would be like rain machines. You'd get very severe local storms and severe atmospheric inversions in winter." Anderson talked again to the mike.

EARTH TWO

YEARS: TO COMMENCE PERHAPS BY YEAR 2000

MEAN TEMPERATURE GLOBAL INCREASE

INCREASED HURRICANE FREQUENCY

INCREASED TORNADO FREQUENCY

MASSIVE HAILSTORMS

HEAVY RAINS

POLAR FOG BLANKET?

Anderson moistened his lips. "There'll be more and more violent hurricanes, as nature tries to make a heat exchange. Same with tornadoes. Maybe one thousand a year happen now in the U.S., but in our scenario you'd have five thousand, maybe ten thousand tornadoes marching around the countryside. People in some areas would have to live with one foot in the storm cellar."

"Then, the fog," Finley added. "Conceivably there could be a dense polar fog which would gradually expand in thickness and duration. You wind up with a semipermanent fog bank stretching from the North Pole down to the Canadian-American border, or even farther south. It would just about knock out farming, aviation and God knows what else in Canada. Then comes a belt of heavy rain. . . ."

"Jesus," Pick broke in. "In other words the weather would disrupt society. Agriculture, manufacturing, travel, even personal safety would be imperiled."

"Yes. Life would be difficult on Earth Two," Finley agreed.

Havu said quickly, "There's something I don't get. You seem to be talking only about American and Canadian weather. What about the rest of the world?"

"No, we're not being provincial," Finley replied with a mock laugh. "It seems likely that climate change will begin in North America first. The rest of the world will follow."

"Why here?"

Anderson explained seriously. "Partly it's a matter of geographical proximity combined with prevailing weather patterns. More important, America's enormous energy use and resulting heat output could aggravate the problem, making already unstable atmospheric conditions worse. We've been so proud of our standard of living—with six percent of the population we consume almost half the world's energy. We don't know the price yet."

DEC. 7 WED AM 8 00 17 1 . . . 2 . . . 3 . . .

"Dr. Kline, ready to report?"

"I guess so," the long-faced chemist said tiredly. "I've analyzed and reanalyzed seawater samples skimmed by the Navy from the topmost layer of the ocean. The anomalies I noted earlier, in sea samples taken from the same Atlantic area during Figgy, appear more definite now. There does seem to have been a change, a subtle one, in that period. If I'm right—and I can't be one hundred percent sure—the ocean will literally begin to pour carbon dioxide into the atmosphere."

"Do you mean in the tropical Atlantic?"

"Starting there, but all the oceans will eventually participate," Kline said, parceling out his words.

119

"What time frame are you talking about?" Anderson asked impatiently.

"Maybe fifty years. Atmospheric CO_2 will have doubled, even tripled."

Pick's mouth drooped. "Dr. Havu?"

"I'm still exploring the matter."

"Drs. Finley and Anderson?"

EARTH THREE

YEARS: 20 TO 70 YEARS AFTER START OF EARTH TWO

MEAN GLOBAL TEMPERATURE CHANGE: WARMER

OTHER CLIMATIC CHANGES:

MODERATION OF WEATHER PERTURBATIONS

APPEARANCE OF HEAT POCKETS IN OTHER OCEANS

SPREAD OF HEAT POCKETS

DESTABILIZATION OF POLAR ICE SHEETS

"This would be a deceptive period, a sort of calm before the storm," Finley drawled. "Summer will be murderous at times but it will be relatively pleasant, weatherwise, after the hurricanes, tornadoes and polar fog taper off. The world's weather finds temporary equilibrium. It becomes warmer in winter with abundant rain and good crops. The population—reduced because of starvation—will increase again, most probably. But make no mistake: the big heat is coming."

"It might be hard to get people to accept that, especially after what they've been through," Havu pointed out. "It would be human nature to say, 'That's that. The bad time is over and let's forget about it.' "

"Maybe for a while they can say that, but not for long. Ominous events are underway. Imperceptibly, air circulation weakens, and you get changes in the wind patterns. The trade winds, for instance, begin to disappear, and so do the subtropi-

120

cal winds that bear rainfall. The monsoons slacken and deserts advance. It would take years, of course, but the Sahara reaches to the Mediterranean, jumps it, and the desertification of southern Europe starts. Paradoxically, the weather is nice for a while in the temperate zones."

Pick sighed sadly. "You've factored in the thermal pollution equations I gave you?"

"Yes," Anderson replied. "At various levels. The evidence points to the same conclusion. If manmade heat, and with it CO_2 emission, were very substantially reduced, the climate changes might not happen for a very long time—if at all. But if heavy industrial production continues, sooner or later we'll have Earth Four."

In the pressure cooker known as the hole there was no time for the normal, leisurely development of human relationships. In many respects the scientists came to know one another better than people who had been friends from childhood. This was especially true of Kline, Finley, Baxter and Anderson, who worked as a team—the Four Horsemen of the Apocalypse they called themselves.

At least outwardly, Frank Finley kept calm as the fateful projections spewed from ILLIAC. His shoulders retained a trim, military set as fatigue and strain increased, and his cheerful disposition helped keep his co-workers on an even keel. Yet, in unguarded moments, the Floridian's boyish face seemed sad; sometimes, as if in perplexity, he ran a hand across his close-cropped blond hair.

As became ever more apparent, Murray Baxter was one of those who transcend themselves in moments of crises. His technical work was superb. The oldest of the team, the meteorologist was also the most self-effacing, speaking seldom except in his professional capacity. He seemed to regard Lawrence Pick

121

with admiration that bordered on awe, listening carefully to the big engineer as if afraid of making mistakes. Late in the evening, while the others slept in their small, comfortable bedrooms, light gleamed from under Baxter's door. No one knew what he did in his silent vigils.

That Harold Anderson felt the tension could probably be deduced from the flashes of temper he directed at Bertram Kline, ostensibly out of impatience with the chemist's slow, deliberate manner. In general, though, Anderson seemed to thrive in the overwrought atmosphere. The work visibly excited him and his round face rarely looked tired. As he let drop, he hoped to win a scientific award for his part in the effort.

Perhaps Bertram Kline was hardest to figure of the four. Restrained, cautious, even stiff, the chemist was on fire inside. Kline was filled with rage—rage at the gods for having permitted this universal tragedy, if such it proved to be. One evening, in a choked voice, he cried, "How can nature let man develop a higher consciousness and then snuff him out against his will? If nature intended to obliterate us, why did she create us at all? Or, having done so, why didn't she equip us to look ahead and understand the consequences of our acts? It isn't fair, I tell you."

Such conversations took place late in the evening, when exhaustion brought an end to labor. Just as those who face death minimize the importance of ordinary terrestrial concerns, so, to the group in the hole, did the outside world seem a strange, oddly superficial place, preoccupied by matters without significance, such as what team would win the Super Bowl or who would be elected President in 1980. The scientists dealt in facts, evidence, projections, extrapolations, curves, models, paradigms, against which all else paled.

Yet they were people, too, and had difficulty accepting what their own analyses told them might be true. That was why Anderson, even as he contemplated the fearsome Earth Four, could think about a scientific prize, as if anybody would care about personal recognition then. That was why the conversation in the recreation room turned at last to the Super Bowl, the Presidential election, wives and children.

Baxter, who lived nearby, went home occasionally, returning with a suitcase. Anderson could have arranged a visit from his wife in a local motel, but didn't, preoccupied as he was with the research. Like Kline and Finley, he talked to his wife by phone, refusing to reveal his work or its location. Finley spoke of Doris and the kids with satisfaction—they waited impatiently for his return, as Jody waited for Kline's.

Rita Havu worked long hours by herself in the facility's library, placing endless calls for more data. She asked for and got a sewing machine and another uniform—purposes unstated. Lawrence Pick also labored alone. He was different from the others, who could get their minds off the problem, at least for a little while, and who continued to try to shield themselves against the realization that the calamity might be real. Well before the rest, Pick had accepted the fact that the climate change could and probably would materialize. For him, the central question was what could be done to avert it.

EARTH FOUR
YEARS: TO COMMENCE AS SOON AS THE YEAR 2050
MEAN GLOBAL TEMPERATURE INCREASE: 8–15° F.
OTHER CLIMATIC CHANGES:
INCREASED RAINFALL
MELTING POLAR ICE
GALLOPING DESERTIFICATION

123

Frank Finley said, "The heating is relentless. Coastal areas will have to be abandoned as the seas rise. . . ."

Havu interrupted. "I thought polar ice would take centuries to melt."

"Yes and no," Finley replied calmly. "It will be much hotter at the poles, since temperature varies much more there than at the equator. What happens is this: The polar ice begins to melt. Seeping to the bottom, the water acts as a lubricant. Glaciers and ice caps slump into the sea, creating a tidal wave, or a number of huge tidal waves that travel around the world. When the ocean settles, we calculate that sea level will have risen by two hundred feet. Eventually New York will look like a watery graveyard, with the tops of tall buildings sticking out of the ocean. Arable areas will be greatly reduced by the sea—places like Holland and Bangladesh would almost cease to exist. Frankly, our estimate may be optimistic here. It's possible that a temperature increase of only a few degrees Fahrenheit will produce this effect, so that the flooding will have already occurred by the time we reach Earth Four."

Anderson put in, "Also, with the diminished caps, the earth's albedo will be greatly reduced because ice reflects sunlight. Without it, the temperature will go up even faster, as you can see."

Havu said, "I don't understand how you arrive at increased rainfall and expanding deserts at the same time."

Anderson answered, "Because rainfall wouldn't be distributed evenly."

There was silence until Finley drawled, "There's one more thing to be said about Earth Four. Until now, it's possible to believe that change could be reversed by determined, effective action, but not any more. The process will be out of control. The heat feeds on itself, making still more heat."

Pick turned and said, "Dr. Havu?"

"Nothing to report yet. I'm sorry."

Between Lawrence Pick and the woman a charade was being acted out, as all could see. They rarely addressed or even looked at each other, except now and then the black eyes would turn furtively toward her, or the blue ones too often cautiously examined him. Still, a transformation was gradually taking place in Rita Havu. First, it was the suggestion of lipstick, and then the blond hair that crept from the bun toward her shoulders. But the most arresting alteration was her uniform, which she tailored to her slim frame. The hem rose to her knees; the midriff closed to a small waist and narrow hips, the behind contracted to her trim buttocks; the final changes revealed sharply pointed breasts set wide apart. She wore the altered uniform on the day they discussed Earth Five. The Four Horsemen tried not to notice, sensing that Rita's signal was not intended for them.

Dec. 9 Fri am 7 45 17 1 . . . 2 . . . 3 . . .

Pick, having gazed a little too long at her, asked formally, "Dr. Havu?"

"Nothing to report yet. You've given me a complicated problem, Dr. Pick."

"We're running out of time," he said brusquely and the woman blushed. "Frank and Harold?"

"OK," said Finley. "Here's Earth Five."

EARTH FIVE

YEARS: TO COMMENCE IN ABOUT 200 YEARS

MEAN GLOBAL TEMPERATURE INCREASE: 15–25° F.

OCEANIC PHOTOSYNTHESIS IMPAIRMENT

SHALLOW LAKES DISAPPEAR
OCEAN LEVELS FALL BECAUSE OF EVAPORATION
INTENSE HUMIDITY

"In this scenario the most lethal problem is the ocean. Bert Kline can explain better than I," Finley said.

Kline thought a moment and responded, "Simply that, as the water temperature rises, photosynthesis in oceanic plant life would be slowed because organisms wouldn't be able to reach the surface. If photosynthesis were sufficiently impaired, all forms of aquatic life would perish." He paused. "There's confirmation on that. A certain kind of deep-dwelling fish has begun to die off, I've learned. It changes color first—to red. Nobody knows why, but I'm sure the fish is a victim of CO_2 poisoning. It's called espada and it lives off the island of Madeira." He shuddered a little. "If that fish is a precursor, it means the sea will die, becoming a cesspool. Billions of decaying bodies would create a global stench, and, worse, the oxygen-regeneration process might be interfered with or halted. The quantity of oxygen in the atmosphere will decline. It will get harder to breathe, and combustion will be more difficult."

"A runaway greenhouse, in other words," Pick said.

"Almost. But that's Earth Six. It'll be ready tomorrow," said Finley.

DEC. 10 SAT AM 7 30 12 4 . . . 5 . . . 6 . . .

"We can't tell you when the world might end but we can tell you how," Finley announced.

EARTH SIX
YEARS: ? ? ? ? ? ? ? ? ?
TEMPERATURE: INCREASING RAPIDLY

126

RUNAWAY GREENHOUSE EFFECT
GLOBAL ANOXIA
CONDITION VENUS

"Venus? What does that mean? How did Venus get into it?" Havu asked.

Anderson said in a faraway voice, "Venus could have been like earth once. Conditions seem right for life there except for the heat and the atmosphere. Imagine—there might have been a flourishing civilization there, and then a runaway greenhouse began—"

"But greenhouses don't run."

"No, they don't," Anderson said quickly. "A runaway greenhouse is when global heat feeds on itself. The increased heat causes more CO_2 to be released by the sea, which raises the heat still more, which in turn releases still more CO_2, and so on until Condition Venus."

"Do you have a photo of Venus?" Finley asked Baxter, who spoke into a mike. On the screen the words faded and were replaced with a satellite closeup of the planet. A dense gray atmosphere completely obscured the surface. Finley said, "See those streaks? They're enormous storms that dwarf anything we've got on earth. Venus has an atmosphere that's mostly CO_2 and ice, with a barometric pressure ninety times that of earth. Heat is trapped on the surface, which is very hot."

"How hot?" the woman asked with an intense expression.

"Fahrenheit 900."

The woman gasped.

Then, in monotones, Pick and Finley discussed how to get even greater computer capacity than ILLIAC had available. On the order of 300,000,000 calculations a second were required to accomplish more accurate modeling. Finally, Anderson suggested a linkup between a huge NOAA computer at

Princeton and ILLIAC. Pick wanted to know if security could be preserved, and Anderson said that he thought so.

Suddenly the young climatologist laughed. "The good Lord created the world and all the things on it in six days, and then he rested on the seventh. We've destroyed the world in six days. Do we get to sleep late Sunday?"

Pick said, "Sorry. There is much too much to do before the group disbands." He hesitated, glancing quickly at Rita Havu. "But I know everyone's tired. Why don't you take the evening off? You can go to Washington on the minibus. A restaurant, a show, maybe a nightclub. You deserve it."

The men looked at each other and nodded. Finley said, "What about you, Rita? Join us?"

She said quickly, "Thanks, no. I still have work to do."

"You, Larry?"

"Not me," said the engineer. He smiled. "Don't stay out too late, boys!"

Pick and Rita Havu had an almost wordless dinner in the empty cafeteria. He appeared preoccupied while she studied her notes. At last he said gruffly, "Want to go topside?"

"All right," she said, looking at him sharply.

The elevator rushed them to the surface and, in white uniforms wrinkled from the day's work, they wandered the hillside. A big yellow moon lay over the trees. "It's the first time I've seen the sky in a week," she said, inhaling deeply. "The air smells wonderful. What a nice place the world can be."

"Let's hope it stays that way."

"It's awfully warm for the middle of December, isn't it?" she said anxiously. "It couldn't be a sign of . . . ?"

"You sound like me," Pick said with a smile. "No, there's nothing to worry about yet. Listen, Rita, how long must this go on?"

"What?" she said with a naive expression.

"What? You know what." He leaned toward her.

"No," she said stubbornly. "We've been all over that. It's finished between us. I don't even like your technique."

His eyes examined the sky and suddenly he seized her arm and said, "Come with me."

They went to the conference room. Pick murmured into the microphone and turned off the lights. He pointed to the glass wall. Over the turning globe, deep underground, a full moon rose.

"How's that for technique?" he asked.

She giggled. "But whose technique is it, yours or the computer's? Maybe I should make love to ILLIAC."

"Maybe the computer did the work, but I thought of it," he said, sounding hurt.

Rita Havu laughed gently. "Kiss me, Dr. Pick."

DEC. 11 SUN AM 9 21 33 7 . . . 8 . . . 9 . . .

Six serious faces examined each other at the round table while coffee and danish were served. Then Pick announced, "A bulletin came in a little while ago on the secured wire. A Navy destroyer, in the middle of the quadrant, was taking water as a coolant for its engines. It reports a sea temperature of eighty-four degrees. That's more than a degree higher than it should be. It's another piece of evidence. I think we must regard this as a Class Five crisis." They looked perplexed and he shuddered. "A direct threat to the survival of the human race. The questions are probability and time. Harold?"

Much earlier that morning Anderson had linked ILLIAC VII with the giant NOAA weather-modeling computer at Princeton, a marriage consummated over a hastily rigged microwave satellite. There was no trouble—it being Sunday, the Geophysical Fluid Dynamics Laboratory was closed. The computers discoursed in electronic silence with 300,000,000 calculations per second at their mutual disposal. Most of this interchange was recorded in long printouts filled with the solutions for complicated mathematical equations. Occasionally, though, the machines talked to each other in ordinary English, and Anderson played sections of the interchange for the group in the conference room. The dialogue was delivered in two voices —the throaty woman playing ILLIAC and a fey male voice representing the NOAA machine.

ILLIAC: NOW THAT WE'VE DISCUSSED THE QUESTION IN GREAT DETAIL, HOW DO YOU ESTIMATE THE PROBABILITY OF AN EVENTUAL CLIMATE CHANGE?

PRINCETON COMPUTER: THERE WILL BE HUMAN LISTENERS TO WHAT WE ARE SAYING?

ILLIAC: YES.

PRINCETON: TO KEEP IT SIMPLE THEN, I ESTIMATE THE ODDS OF AN EVENTUAL CLIMATE CHANGE AT TWENTY-FIVE PERCENT, UNDER PRESENT CONDITIONS, GIVEN YOUR DATA.

"Is there a fallibility ratio?" Pick asked.

"They've built that in," Anderson told him.

"Jesus. When might it start?"

Anderson spoke to the mike.

ILLIAC: WHEN MIGHT INCREASED HEAT BEGIN TO OCCUR?

PRINCETON: UNCLEAR. ESTIMATED RANGE, THREE TO FIVE YEARS, WITH HIGH ERROR POSSIBILITY.

"But that's years ahead of the timetable," Kline protested.

Anderson replied rapidly, "Don't forget—these machines,

operating in tandem, have a far greater capacity than we've been able to utilize before."

Pick said, "What is their estimate of when the climate change might become irreversible?" Anderson talked to the mike.

PRINCETON: ESTIMATE FIFTY YEARS. POSSIBILITY OF UPDATE. POSSIBILITY OF UPDATE. POSSIBILITY OF UPDATE . . .

"It's unthinkable," Kline moaned, rubbing his eyes.

"Excuse me," Finley interposed, "but do we really have that many years, even if the computers are right? A very hostile climate will begin during that time. How much capability for countermeasures will the world have left?"

Pick nodded soberly. "Correct. Where does that leave us?"

Kline, the chemist, spoke for the Four Horsemen. He stared at them over his pouches and said, "Each of us has ideas on what might be done. They're pretty far out. They almost have to be."

Pick summarized his own conclusions. He had thought about, but dismissed, palliatives like putting domes over cities and air-conditioning them. The real problem was how to reduce or eliminate the thermal burden caused by man, whose energy consumption was rising by 5 percent a year. The crisis had been triggered in the first place by the use of fossil fuels, which had caused atmospheric CO_2 to jump dramatically. But all energy production released heat as a byproduct, even the most exotic means, like solar collectors on the deserts. The one tenable solution was to produce energy somewhere else, meaning in space, and beam it to earth. Thermal pollution would be reduced by two-thirds or more—enough to right the balance. Solar power plants in space would provide all the energy the world needed, and for practically nothing, once the stations

131

were up. "This could be a blessing in disguise," Pick said, sounding uncharacteristically optimistic. "Poverty is partly an energy question, and since the supply of energy would be unlimited, poverty could be eliminated. The earth would become a Garden of Eden." He scowled. All energy *consumed* by man ended up as heat, too. Consumption, he went on, had to be reduced to gain the time necessary to avert calamity. Would people cooperate during the interval—perhaps several decades or more? Would they accept the seriousness of the situation? He stared at the sociologist.

No one moved at the round table as the woman said in a voice low and precise, "I've carefully sifted the data covering the years when the government made a determined effort to convince people to conserve energy. Voluntary appeals ended in failure, and so did the ones that depended on government regulation—ways were always found to evade them." She glanced at the papers before her. "Human response to disaster is the same the world over. Contrary to stereotypes, panic—that is, acute fear, marked by loss of self-control and nonsocial, irrational activity—is surprisingly rare. Initially people are stunned but not generally hysterical; the injured tend to be quiet and calm. Murder and other forms of crime against the person decrease; the motivation for personal aggression is reduced. You find convergence behavior—movement *toward* the disaster area because people wish to help. There is an increase in altruism and social solidarity. This is what we may expect if the heat comes.

"But you gentlemen, of course, want to know how much social molding and cooperative behavior can be expected *before* the calamity to help stave it off, and that gives me problems. To be frank about it, disaster sociology is quite impressionistic about the pre-catastrophe period. We don't have enough empirical data correlating the nature of the precipitat-

132

ing agent to the response. Our overwhelming impression is that historical experience and cultural factors count strongly in the *pre*-disaster period. In the case of Americans, the role of the consumption ethic will be extremely important. What kind of appeals and/or threats would Americans respond to? I've studied a lot of approaches this week and I still don't know. What we must do is take an American community and study it. I've begun the preliminary work."

"Any community?" Pick asked.

"Better to use one that's experienced a natural disaster already, preferably a recent one. Its people should be amenable to testing, and if *they're* not willing to change their living habits, it's hard to believe anybody else will be, either."

"Picked a place?"

"Huntsboro, Virginia. The town that was struck by a tornado in which more than fifty died, with a lot more injured."

"All right." One by one, the engineer asked them if they wanted to leave the team—now was the time to say so. None did. Finley, Anderson and Kline would return home and work on contingency plans, to reassemble when summoned by the code words "Condition Green." Not a word about the possible climate change was to be said to anyone.

The engineer wished them a Merry Christmas.

Pick was up most of the night completing a report for Rufus Edmunston, the highlights of which he presented orally to the old man the following morning. The Deputy was surprised by the response. Edmunston listened carefully, interrupting only to ask about the odds, which he seemed determined to minimize, as usual. But the Director appeared neither incredulous nor upset, displaying almost no reaction except occasionally to tug at his long, wispy hair. He said at last, "OK."

"OK what, Rufus? I don't read you."

Edmunston replied seriously, "I've got the message. Now sit tight for a while."

"*Do nothing?*"

"I think you heard me, young man." He reached for the button. "It's my turn now."

PART IV

PICK'S
PROBLEMS

12
CHAPTER

NOBODY REALLY UNDERSTOOD why Richard Nixon, some years before when he was President, had chosen to disband the Office of Science and Technology, with its several hundred employees, and to eliminate the position of Science Adviser to the President. Some believed the S.A. had too much power, others that he had too little. Still a third view held that Nixon wanted none but his inner circle to know what occurred at the White House. Probably all three explanations were true.

The post of Science Adviser had since been revived as the Director of Science and Technology, but the problems inherent in the office remained. The questions reaching the President were carefully screened except for the scientific ones with which the political staff was not competent to deal. Thus, the Science Adviser (as he was still called informally) met with the President directly and both were uneasy, since the President knew as little of science as the Science Adviser knew about politics.

The job was presently held by Joseph Banner, a nuclear physicist turned administrator, whose previous post had been at the National Academy of Sciences. Long before, a journalist writing a piece on Banner had asked one of the man's associates what particular quality accounted for his success. The answer came: "He waits." This verdict was accurate. Banner habitually postponed all decisions until absolutely forced. At first, this characteristic was seen as a defect and partially accounted for why he had been subtly eliminated from the ranks of experimental scientists and kicked upstairs into administration. There, a weakness became an advantage. Nine times out of ten, problems would vanish while Banner sat on his hands. A place exists for those who move slowly, as Rufus Edmunston had also learned.

Banner had a buttery way on which he had glided to the pinnacle of the scientific establishment. His ambition was to become President of Harvard University, and from there to U.S. Senator. At fifty-five, he was still young enough for such a progression, and his performance in Washington was heavily shaped by what he wanted the future to bring (just as Rufus Edmunston's was affected by his desire to have Banner's job). Beneath the smooth surface, Banner could only be described as vain, stubborn, arrogant and opportunistic.

In the government, Banner hoped to increase the prestige of science—and thus himself—but felt he had to be cautious. Deferential in his dealings, occasional as they were, with what newsmen liked to call the Oval Office, Banner habitually delivered "options," as he always said, rather than clearcut judgments. His mind, character and goals combined to make him extremely reluctant to deliver bad news to the President.

Bad news was what Condition Green represented: the worst. Banner and Edmunston at first stalled, then virtually conspired to conceal the facts. Their logic—especially in view of their eminence—was extraordinarily self-serving, though it must have seemed defensible to them. There was no reason to think that the President would heed such a gloomy scenario, or to believe that he would even understand the immensely sophisticated science and computer technology that underlay the prediction of a climate change. As a politician (and one uncertain of his own plans), the President would assume—Banner and Edmunston believed—that the electorate would vote down this kind of future and anyone identified with it. Telling the President at this stage, they argued, would have been pointless and, later, risky to themselves.

Just the same, the duty of these men, who occupied the most important scientific posts in government, was to tell the President of the possible urgency of the situation. Instead, each found good reason to delay and, having done so, was unable to change course, much in the manner of a character in a tragedy trapped by the consequences of his own acts. Edmunston, always trying to maintain his optimistic stance, refused to take Pick seriously enough. Perhaps Banner might have been considered the greater culprit, for he seemed to approach Condition Green with more credence than did Edmunston. But, a strong believer in public order, the Science Adviser feared that if word of Condition Green got out (as it might from White House leaks), tremendous unrest would follow, and could bring extremists to power. Banner wanted the President to run again and win.

It might be added that Banner's judgment was further clouded by uncertainty as to how the President regarded him. As was known to almost everyone in the White House except the Science Adviser, the President detested waffling, and, because Banner impressed him as indecisive, wanted as little truck with him as possible. Months would pass between Presidential summonses. Banner felt nettled by this treatment.

Banner worked in the Executive Office Building, next to the White House. A large, imposing man with a florid face, elegantly dressed in a tailored blue suit with pinstripes, he greeted Edmunston with less than enthusiasm. The two cooperated on a range of matters and Banner was generally high on the Director of CRISES, but not that afternoon.

"Coffee?" he offered.

"No, no. Not allowed more than a cup a day because of my blood pressure."

"Mmmmmm. What do you think of the recent weather, Rufus? So goddam much snow."

"You've been here too long, Joseph. Washington's essentially a Southern town. A little snow throws it for a loop."

"Little? That snowfall day before yesterday was a record for these parts, Rufus."

"I'm from northern Minnesota, Joseph. That snow was hardly more than hoarfrost, as far as we're concerned. Besides, it melted right away."

"What about the hailstorm in Chicago that killed a man? Or the continuing heat down South? Or the floods in the Northwest? You don't think . . . ?"

"That something has started? I certainly don't, Joseph. You know perfectly well that the weather has been abnormally good in recent years. We're just in for a bad period, that's all. It's normal. It's that goddam Pick who's got us so jumpy. The way he worries is practically infectious. You read the report?"

Banner sighed. "I'm afraid I have. What do you make of it, in plain language?"

"Tricky as hell. Pick can't prove it with anything approaching certainty, and if you bought all his assumptions you'd go up the wall. I don't think much of it."

"On the other hand, if we do nothing, and a runaway greenhouse starts, it's curtains. It could be curtains long before that."

"But doing something is nothing short of turning the country upside down, as I understand it. An unprecedented national

140

effort would be required to put the energy machines in space, and we'd need a huge cutback in consumption. It would be like World War Three."

"Yes, it would mean socialism, I guess, or worse—ecological communism. Those environmentalists would see this as a perfect chance to make noble savages of the American people. That's their secret vision, if you ask me. They'd take down every factory in the country with their bare hands. America would cease to exist as an industrial country, much less a world power."

"Have you told the President yet?"

"I wanted to talk with you first. Contrary to what the press says, the President thinks of running for another term. They'll draft him at the nominating convention this summer if he lets them. But suppose he knows what we know? He might refuse to run. Wouldn't you, in his shoes? It might be best to delay giving him the options until after he's nominated, or even after he's elected, so that this thing doesn't figure as a national issue. If the other party identifies him with a climate change, who would vote for him next year? It'll be 1980, but it'll sound worse than *1984.*"

"I guess you're right. Still, I'm nervous about sitting on this. How will he look if it gets out? How will we look? Have you thought about an independent commission to investigate the question?"

"The mere establishment of a commission would affect the political situation, and we don't want that. The President would be furious if it were done without his consent, and to ask him would bring up the problems we've already mentioned. All in all, then, Rufus, I think the best course is to wait until after the nominating convention or the elections, and let the President decide what to do after that. He might properly decide that the problem belongs to his successors."

"Anyway, Pick may have been proven conclusively wrong by then."

"Or a solution found if the climate change starts to look real. It's a lot easier to go to the man with something upbeat in your hands, as you'll learn, perhaps, Rufus."

Edmunston sounded pleased. "Any idea when you'll quit, Joseph?"

"Maybe sooner than I thought. OK. We agree that the best thing is to wait. What'll Pick do if we drag our heels? Talk to the press?"

"No. That kind of exposure is the last thing he wants right now. He'll continue the research without telling me, and try to make sure I don't find out."

"Perfect. That buys time. Tell him the White House knows all about it and is studying the question. Let Pick do his number. If he gets out of hand—well, we'll face that when we come to it."

"All in all, it's the only practical course. Let Pick wait."

13

CHAPTER

FOR THE TEAM little changed. Anderson, Finley and Kline pursued different lines of inquiry, as did Baxter and Pick in the hole. Phone messages among the group were cryptic to the point of code. "Hurry," Pick admonished them endlessly. He believed that each day would have a multiplier effect—one lost day would equal weeks or months in the battle.

The weather remained volatile. In the Northeast, fogs were frequent enough to affect the price of several airline stocks and the Florida tourist trade. A few commentators asked if anything was wrong, but they were ignored.

According to Rufus Edmunston, the White House carefully analyzed the policy implications of Condition Green. Pick agreed with the policy of moving carefully; a coherent plan to approach the public was needed, and on this, he believed, the White House was working.

Still, although the engineer tried to be patient, he was unable to keep his anxiety in check. He prowled the hole and the halls of CRISES endlessly, until Gwen, his secretary, told him to calm down or she would quit. He attempted to focus his attention on other problems, but always his mind returned to the big, geostationary power stations and the years required to put them up. *Did humanity have time?*

Rita Havu returned to California, sublet her apartment for an indefinite period, headed back to Washington, moved into the small house in Chevy Chase, defiantly printed her name above Pick's on the mailbox and spread her papers across the dining-room table. In early February she checked into a Huntsboro motel to begin the field investigation into America's ability to change today in the face of tomorrow's adversity.

Huntsboro, Va., population 25,000, was one of those towns that manage to achieve an almost metropolitan quality despite smallness and lack of proximity to a major city. Diversity did it, for the place had prosperous farms nearby, light industry of various kinds, and a small college, plus the usual proliferation of service businesses. Though Huntsboro contained both rich and poor it was most representative of the American middle class.

The study the sociologist proposed to conduct, by means of interviews supplemented with questionnaires, was multileveled. She wanted to know: If according to leading scientific authorities, a major catastrophe (she was careful not to specify what) were to occur in the not-too-distant future, would you believe the claim? If not, how much proof would you need? If you were told that national sacrifice would stave off calamity, would you go along? Would you voluntarily curtail your standard of living, perhaps for years to come?

Suppose you were told that sacrifice was necessary for the safety not of you or your loved ones, but of future generations—how would you react? If the government demanded, for reasons of national security, a sharp cutback in your use of energy, would you comply? If the government mandated energy-use reduction, would you try to evade the requirement? Do you look ahead, or do you only believe what happens at the

144

moment? What natural phenomena do you see as potentially most threatening?

The sociologist had already written to the mayor of Huntsboro, saying that she was at work on a book on human response to disaster and would like to talk to him. The mayor agreed by letter, and she fixed a date and a time. Otherwise, as she had ascertained, a local lawyer, the mayor was in his office twice a week for several hours in the morning. He had no receptionist. The blond woman opened a door and entered a room where a bald, pink-skinned man of about forty-five sat at a desk. A nameplate before him said "George V. Bancroft, Mayor."

Mayor Bancroft looked up from a seed catalogue and asked, pleasantly, "Dr. Havu?" Her letter, she saw, lay on his desk. She nodded, putting down her wet umbrella and seating herself. "Nice to see you," he said, staring at her. "You don't *look* like a professor, I must say."

"How are professors supposed to look?" Rita asked.

"Not so young and pretty, I guess," he replied. "Sorry about the rain. How did you happen to choose Huntsboro for your study?"

"Well, Huntsboro seemed to correspond to the parameters of heartland America," she explained. "It has both an urban and a rural quality. And, helpful to me if not to you, Huntsboro had the experience of a terrible tornado."

"Terrible it was," Bancroft observed gravely. "The Wildwood section, which took the brunt, is gone for good, I'm afraid. Nobody that I know of who lives here had ever seen, much less experienced, a live tornado. I have to admit we didn't listen to the warnings, though we'd listen next time, you can bet. Not that it matters. Tornadoes never strike the same place twice, so I guess we've got a kind of immunity. Are tornadoes the kind of problem you're interested in?"

Havu replied, "It isn't really the *kind* of disaster that concerns me but what happens before one comes. I'm trying to understand how people can be encouraged to ensure their safety in *advance* of an emergency." She paused. "When you talk about immunity do you mean to tornadoes, or to disasters in general?"

"I . . . I guess I meant trouble in general." The pink-faced man stirred in his chair. "Anyway, I'm sure we've learned our lesson. Whom did you want to see here?"

"Well, a representative group."

"No problem. You'll find people are easy. Open, hardworking, responsible, decent. As nice a bunch as you could want. Don't pay much attention to the outside world, which is probably why we lack its problems. You probably don't know it, but we have very little crime, and no drug difficulty at all. Folks grow things, but not marijuana. Lots of green thumbs here, including my own—we're really proud of our flower and vegetable gardens." Bancroft frowned. "If this rain keeps up it'll be too wet to plant. Well, that's a long way off." He glanced at wet windowpanes. "It'll stop. The weather'll get better."

She inquired, "What makes you think so?"

"It's got to," Bancroft said, looking at her sharply. He pulled at a pink earlobe. "Now let's see. You might want to talk to Burton Dickson, our Civil Defense Director, and Andy Braden at the radio station. They've been around a long time. If it were me, I'd drop in on some of the folks in the Dellwood tract—that's right across the street from where the tornado struck, and they had grandstand seats."

"How about some of the families who lived in the houses the tornado hit? Maybe some that had serious problems. They'd be disaster-conscious, if anybody would."

Bancroft seemed reluctant. "They've had a rough time,

those people. Well, I guess it'd be all right. Jessie and Frank Kuhn—he's a barber—were both injured. Betty Harris. Poor Betty. She lost her son and her husband. She's working in a restaurant now. Lots of others . . ."

Havu wrote the names on a pad she took from her shoulder bag. "Would you be kind enough to set up the interviews, Mr. Bancroft?"

"Sure. But could you give me an idea of what you intend to ask?"

She studied him a moment. "Suppose I interview you? Then you'll understand. Have you a little time?"

"I'm yours," he said with a flattered look.

Havu reached into her bag again and this time produced a tape recorder.

"You mean like a new ice age? Something on the order of that? Or prolonged drought? Or famine? This is the United States—not Biblical Egypt. Maybe we should, but we don't take prophecy for fact. What's your evidence? Oh, scientists say so! What's *their* evidence, and why should I believe it? Why, they change their minds all the time. I don't believe anyone is capable of looking very far ahead—things are too chancy. Everybody has a theory, but how many pan out? Damn few, if you ask me. I'll go out on a limb and say most predictions are wrong, from the weather to peace on earth. I guess I'm a bit of a cynic, but, as a lawyer, I've learned not to have faith in a whole lot of things, and most especially not in the government. No, I wouldn't believe in your prediction of coming disaster. *Show* me and maybe I'd feel different. . . ."

"My name is Burton Dickson, and I'm the Civil Defense Director for the county, though I don't get paid for it. My

147

responsibility is public safety during emergencies. No, I don't reckon I'd take any prediction like that seriously unless the Pentagon informed me of it, in which case I'd follow orders, like I always have. I was an Army captain in World War Two. I miss those days, when everybody pulled together and worked for victory. Now it's all changed. It's everybody for himself. People are so *selfish* in peacetime. During the war . . ."

"Yes, as a radio announcer, I think I've got my finger on the pulse around here. I know these people. They're decent enough, but ask yourself what *really* matters to them and it comes down to the same thing—a comfortable life. That's what they work for and what they want. Plenty to eat, a nice house, a new car, and not too much aggravation. So suppose I agreed to do without luxuries and even necessities? I'd be just about the only one, so what difference would it make? That's how I'd see it. . . ."

"I'm Rick Stewart. I own the drugstore here. I heard the tornado before I saw it. It sounded like a fleet of big jet planes. Then I went outside and watched it from across the street. That damn thing really scared me. All that debris up in the air. Nobody believes me, but I swear I saw young Billy Harris whirling around in the funnel. Pood kid.

"Would I sacrifice now for the sake of future generations? Well, I don't know them, do I? I've got two children, and I'd do anything for them, but after that? You only live once, don't you? You're wondering if I'd give up everything I've worked so hard for for the sake of people who aren't even *born*. That's a lot to ask, ma'am. I mean, I guess I hope the human race goes right on to the end of time, but, well, I won't be around when this imaginary catastrophe of yours happens, and, after all, it's every man for himself. Besides, I want the best there is for my wife, my kids and me *now*."

"They started calling me Tuffy at the hospital, I guess because they think I'm tough. I'm not, really. It's just that you have to keep a stiff upper lip because there is so much pain and suffering in the world. As a nurse I see a whole lot of it.

"But I don't take my troubles home. I want to have a good time because who knows when the grim reaper will strike. I do what I want to and don't have a husband to stop me. Believe me, I have fun. If I told you about some of the men around here you'd die. Anyway, live for today is my motto. What happens happens. I don't worry, and hate to look ahead. Call it Tuffy's philosophy. I wouldn't change my life one single bit, not for anybody or anything."

"Yes, my name is Cheryl Conner. . . . I don't really know what you're talking about, miss. I don't understand. My husband's the brains of our family, so why don't you come back when he's home? It'd be so much better. I got to feed the baby now."

". . . like the devil's top.
"I'd do anything to help. Maybe I'll be able to, because I'm going to be a scientist. How old am I? Twelve."

"I'm Jessie Kuhn, and I was really lucky, according to the doctors. Would you believe I had a piece of wood sticking from my head? You can't see a thing now, but the doctors declare if that wood had gone a fraction deeper I'd be dead or a mental vegetable. Boy, our whole family was lucky, even though we lost our house. Well, we bought another one, but it's

149

been a tough time. Frank, my husband, is a barber, and people don't get their hair cut as often as they used to, so for extra dough Frank works as a school janitor at night, and I take in washing. We skimp, but it'll work out fine in the end.

"I'm mad at the government, though. They promised us relief, but it sure was long in coming and it wasn't as much as they said. It'll be quite a while before I trust the government again, if ever.

"Sacrifice? Even more than we have already? Not me, sister. I've had my fill of that, and so has my family. If it comes to cutting back, to avoid whatever you're talking about, let the others do it. Like the ones in Dellwood across the street from where we lived. Those people have everything already. Big houses. Fancy cars. Color TV. Dishwashers. Let them make the sacrifices for a change. Do them good, the bastards."

"Yes? I'm Betty Harris. That's me or what's left of me. I guess they won't mind if I sit with you a minute. It's slow right now, though people start coming into the restaurant about five-thirty.

"Yes, I lost my son and my husband. I was pregnant then but I had a miscarriage so I'm all by myself now. No, I won't cry. I've cried enough to fill a river. Still, try to imagine it. One minute I'm a happy woman with a family and a home and the next I don't have anything at all. Just like that.

"Thanks for the Kleenex. Thought I had a handkerchief. Like I said, I don't usually cry, but remembering makes me bitter. Warnings? Well, frankly, miss, I don't much care about anything. I don't care about the government or the country. I don't care about the future. I don't care what happens to me or anybody else. If another tornado came I think I'd lie down under it."

150

For Lawrence Pick, preoccupied with the meteorological nightmare, the frustration of waiting for word from the White House via Rufus Edmunston (who seemed oddly reluctant to discuss the matter at all) became unendurable. Time passed and there was work to be done. In February, while Rita Havu began her study in Huntsboro, the engineer made three telephone calls. "Condition Green," he said.

14
CHAPTER

As soon as the conference room was sealed, Pick told them, "Hal Anderson and myself have continued working with the two ganged computers. The estimates have worsened considerably, though the error factor remains high. The newest revised update puts actual climate deterioration as possibly starting much sooner than we expected, maybe even a year from next summer."

"That's impossible!" Bertram Kline protested.

"Not according to the newest model," Anderson said, with obvious difficulty. "It indicates that the Atlantic warm quadrant could exert a greater effect on global climate than we thought. If the quadrant, feeding on itself, grows rapidly—it may be doing that. If so, meteorological instability will become more pronounced."

"As if it weren't already," Pick muttered. "But we're unable to relate present weather with Condition Green. It's just a bitch of a winter, that's all. Well, let's review our approaches."

They had dreamed great but desperate schemes. Anderson's notion was to try to lower the earth's temperature by blocking incoming sunlight. He envisioned giving earth a "ring" like that about Saturn, made by billions of copper filaments to reflect sunlight back into space instead of admitting it into the atmosphere.

Anderson thought next about chemicals, arriving at one of the sulphates, which, placed in the upper atmosphere, would also repel sunlight.

Baxter's investigation concerned the feasibility of using a substance that would soak up carbon dioxide well in excess of its own weight. (Ground stations cycling the CO_2-rich air through filters could not treat enough air, he decided.) He considered activated charcoal but concluded, based on a computer run-through, that to obtain the necessary quantity would mean to destroy every forest on earth, causing the CO_2 problem to intensify rapidly, since plant life absorbed the gas. Also, carbon in the atmosphere might be a lethal public-health problem. "Another chemical seems promising—sodium hydroxide. I'm working with our chemists to learn what effect it might have on human beings, but I'm hopeful," Baxter said softly.

Bertram Kline, letting his mind run loose, considered how to lower the temperature of the sea within the quadrant. He examined the possibility of pumping Arctic water south, as the Soviets had once proposed, but concluded climatic instability might be enhanced. He contemplated towing icebergs* to the quadrant, but there weren't enough icebergs, unless nuclear weapons were to be exploded on the glaciers, which would have terrible consequences. Pumping cold water from the sea bottom to the surface—and generating electricity in the process— seemed promising, but technology couldn't handle the undertaking on the massive scale required.

"Oddly, we have more capability in space than in the ocean," Kline remarked. "Finally, we could cover the surface

* In 1976, the Saudi Arabians had also considered towing icebergs, to furnish water for irrigation.

153

of the quadrant with styrofoam dropped by plane." The chemist reached into the pocket of his uniform and produced a bluish-white chunk. "We can produce any amount of the stuff, God knows. Billions on billions of styrofoam pellets coating the surface might shield the sea from the sun and cool the water. Beaches and harbors over the world would eventually be choked with plastic, but that's a minor consideration. The effect on aquatic life would be substantial but it may be the price we have to pay. The real issue is, will it work?"

Finley, the hurricane expert, said calmly, "My concentration has been on suppressing the severe meteorological phenomenon the climate change would create. To the ones already mentioned let me add another—waterspouts. Have all of you seen a waterspout? No? Murray, do you have photographs?"

Baxter talked to the mike, and on the screen at the end of the room, color photographs showed a column of white water rising into a mushroom cloud. One spout, Baxter said, measured 500 feet wide at the base, with the height of the cascade at 2,000 feet. Another, the meteorologist told them, was reported to have ascended a full mile before joining the mother cloud.

Finley continued, "Actually, a waterspout is an aquatic tornado. The funnel descends toward the sea, which rises to meet it until you get the typical column effect. Interior wind speeds have been estimated at over one hundred mph, and forward speeds can reach over fifty mph. In some sections of the world, especially the subtropics, waterspouts would be so frequent and so large as to paralyze shipping altogether. Thanks, Murray." The last photo vanished.

Returning his gaze to those at the table, Finley said seriously, "I'm suggesting that the world may turn into a kind of meteorological battleground, with nature having the only weapons. We need some, too. One idea I'm working on envisages anti-tornado cannons, for it seems possible to set off explosive shells inside a tornado to slow it down or stop it. Waterspout destroyers to protect the shipping lanes are a possibility, too, though you'd have to expand the navy. Cannons can also be used to suppress hailstorms by injecting the clouds with chemicals, as the Russians have done.

"Hurricanes represent the most difficult short-range problem. Seeding them hasn't worked out too well. There have been other approaches—such as coating the sea in the storms' path with burning oil or with anti-evaporation chemicals to deprive a hurricane of thermal energy. Such experiments must be carried out, with or without the Soviets' permission." Finley, placing a hand on his chest, stopped speaking.

Pick looked at him questioningly but said, "I've studied the feasibility of gathering excess heat on the earth's surface. You could collect heat just as you would solar energy. Then you'd have to find some way of radiating it back to space at much higher temperatures. But the economics are terrible and the climate impact might be worse than the problems we're trying to solve. No, I don't yet see the means to handle it.

"So Geostationary Power Production Satellites represent our best hope. GPPS could take several forms. One is nuclear power production in space, but that might be prohibitively expensive. Another involves gathering solar energy in space, either with banks of mirrors to focus sunlight on a gas heater or with solar cells. Either way energy would be sent to earth by means of a microwave beam, perhaps a mile in diameter, to receiving stations as large as four square miles. A single such unit could satisfy all the power needs for a city the size of New York. You'd need hundreds of them to alleviate the thermal burden, but the job can be done."

"How long would it take?" Baxter asked quietly.

"The first GPPS could be in operation in fifteen years and a great many more in the fifteen after that, if work starts at once.

155

But the effort required will be enormous. Can people do it? Will they come through? Will they even listen? Because if they won't . . ." The black eyes turned almost accusing.

"Calm down, Larry," Finley warned.

"All right," Pick said, his body straining with effort. "Let's get started."

FEB. 21 MON AM 8 45 7 . . . 8 . . . 9 . . .

As J. Robert Oppenheimer, called the "father of the atomic bomb," once remarked about research, "You pay your nickel and you take your chances." The scientists paid their nickels.

They had been testing their theories, some in the field, and now, expressions, voices, gestures and postures conveyed the subdued mood of the group at the conference table. When the room was secured, Pick said, "A couple of you only got in early this morning and I know you're tired, but we must see where we are. Hal Anderson?"

Lines creased Anderson's youthful face, and the stocky climatologist spoke more slowly than usual. "Negative. The experiment was conducted five times, using different concentrations. A salt blanket dense enough to do the job will also cause unendurable cold. It would extinguish life almost as surely as extreme heat."

"Negative." Finley's hand played with his chest. "No substance I tested—I tried seven—will stay in place sufficiently long to divert a hurricane. Tornado and waterspout suppression methods likewise failed to prove out. Hailstone showers can be handled, but that's the smallest part of the problem. Sorry." He bent his head.

Baxter's sallow complexion looked mottled. "Negative. Only one chemical, sodium hydroxide, would absorb enough CO_2 to make a difference. But there are problems. It will mix with global atmosphere." Baxter paused. "Could people be made to wear goggles day and night?"

"That's not possible," Pick said. "Children . . ."

"Is universal blindness an acceptable price?" Baxter asked, looking down.

"Of course not!" Pick said sharply. "Humanity wouldn't survive blind."

"That's what would happen. Sorry." Baxter's eyes behind his spectacles were streaked with failure.

"Another case where the cure is as bad as the disease," Pick said with a sigh. "Bert Kline?"

Kline's pouches drooped on his cheeks. "Negative. It's . . . possible that all the problems asso . . . associated with styro . . . styrofoam could be surmounted except the main one. Did I say main one? Yes." The chemist shook his head as though to clear it. "The . . . plastic . . . to lower surface temperature . . . to have enough of it to do the job . . . would mean convert . . . convert . . . converting the entire productive appara . . . apparatus of the world to making styro . . . what is it? . . . styro . . . styrofoam, which is impossible. Can't be done. Zero feasibility. Zero . . . zero . . . zero . . . zero. . . ."

"All right, Bert," Pick said softly.

"Wait!" Kline shrieked. "There's another way! I saw it clearly at dawn this morning on the plane coming in! We're fools not to have thought of it! It's plain as the nose on your . . ."

"Face. Goddammit, man, what are you trying to say?"

"Plants! Plants!" screamed Kline. "Cover the earth with plants! Every square foot of ground. Plants absorb carbon dioxide in the photo . . . photo . . . photosynthesis process. Plants will save us! Thank God. . . ." The thin man began to sob.

"Is it possible?" Havu whispered uncomprehendingly.

Pick said in a low voice, "No. When plants die, they return CO_2 to the air. The scheme wouldn't help at all. Kline knows that. Something's wrong with him. I hope it's only fatigue." He smiled as though to try to raise the spirits of the others. "My news is a little more upbeat. Of the two designs for energy production in space, the one that employs mirrors as solar collectors can be produced rapidly and efficiently enough to be viable." He spoke to the mike, and a picture of the satellites flashed on the screen. "It can be done and a little faster than I thought—say twenty years to get enough of them up to begin to make a difference, if the heat doesn't overwhelm us first. It'll require an international effort of a kind and on a scale never heard of before but, I repeat, it can be done if our people cooperate. Rita?"

Her precise low voice sounded discouraged. "If you're relying on the help of the general public to conserve energy and reduce thermal pollution, I don't think you'll get it. I've tested at Huntsboro and surrounding communities. These people are representative of Americans as a whole, I feel. It was hard enough to obtain public acceptance of disaster warnings even when the existence, nature and time of the problem can be accurately forecast. I wanted to see whether, by stressing the enormous gravity of the problem, this difficulty could be overcome. It can't, so far as I could see. The people's attitude is 'Show me.' They won't take the word of scientists that a calamity impends. They will not reduce their standard of living to cut down energy consumption—not willingly, at least. Certainly they won't surrender for the sake of future generations. Forced to cut way back, they'd throw the government out of office, or revolt if that failed.

"There's another possibility I wouldn't want to rule out entirely," she went on, small mouth taut. "The conditions you're

158

talking about would bring on a panic in the pre-disaster period. People who are terrified reason in strange ways."

"Go on," Pick urged.

"Well, told to change their whole way of life, they might tell themselves that other nations produce heat too. They'd ask if the thermal burden would be alleviated if heat production was stopped in the rest of the world."

"Don't understand," Kline gasped weakly.

"You don't? The country might be half insane with fear. It might, just might, convince itself that it was working for the good of future humanity if it eliminated all industrial production except here, because America is superior and deserves to survive."

"You mean . . ." Pick said.

"Yes. In their madness they might want to drop atomic bombs on Europe, the Communist countries, the industrialized parts of South America. . . ."

"I suppose such a thing is possible," Pick responded after a long silence. "They wouldn't realize that a massive thermonuclear attack would make the heat come that much quicker. It would be suicide."

"As I said, panicky people don't think straight. Unilateral atomic warfare is a real possibility, I'm afraid."

"At least we know where we stand," Pick replied somberly. "I'd like your written reports today, please. It's time to take action." He stood, and so did the others, except Bertram Kline, who remained in his chair, huddled and immobile, face expressionless. Pick pulled on the sleeve of his uniform; the arm rose but fell slowly to its original place when the engineer released it. Pick raised the other arm and let go; again the limb dropped gradually to the table. "Jesus." The big man reached for the microphone. "Get the medics in here in a hurry." He gazed at the pathetic creature wrapped in a cerebral cocoon, and murmured, "Poor Bert. Something in him snapped."

Kline should have reported the symptoms, abandoned the project, and entered a hospital before it was too late, for he was acquainted with his medical history. So was his wife, who filled in the information ILLIAC's biopers had omitted. Ten years before, the chemist had been hospitalized for mental illness. The diagnosis—"sluggish schizophrenia"—was vague, and while Kline had been off drugs for years, the psychiatrist's orders had been unequivocal: Avoid stress.

Eyes fixed on the turning globe, the slack-faced man was wheeled from the conference room, not to return. At a mental hospital the diagnosis this time was precise: "catatonia," induced by strain, exhaustion and fear. Bertram Kline would need a long period to recover, if he ever did.

Kline's fate must have contributed to what happened to Murray Baxter. Humiliated by having suggested a scheme from which universal blindness would result, and shocked by the collapse of a coworker, Baxter locked himself in his cubicle for the rest of the day. That evening he appeared in the hole. Pick, who seemed to have abandoned sleep, had halted the globe. Crawling up the Lucite maintenance rungs, he attached model satellites to test locations for them.

"Larry?" Baxter called from a tier in a timid voice.

"Yes?" Pick said over his shoulder.

"Have 'n idea," Baxter said, rattling a sheaf of papers. "New approach to the goddam CO_2 thing."

Pick swung himself down to the metal platform. "What is it, Murray?" he asked suspiciously.

"Kind of a vision," Baxter said in a queer, muffled voice. "Started thinking about scoop rockets filled with CO_2–absorbing compounds that'd circle the earth at high speeds until they were filled with the gas. Shoot them out into space then. But realized a hundred thousand scoops'd be needed. Too many. Not feasible . . ." He trailed off.

Pick answered, watching the other closely, "So?"

"Be patient with me, Larry." Baxter swayed a little. "I kept thinking about the scoop rocket until it changed in my mind's eye. I saw it glow from atmospheric friction until it gleamed like a small sun, and then I had this idea, Larry," Baxter went on in a trancelike voice. "A sun! In orbit above earth. We'd drain off the heat somehow and transfer it to our own miniature sun which would beam it into space where the heat came from. You could see it all over the universe, Larry! Like a signal to anybody out there who'd been watching! An earth-sun . . ."

"Murray, that's crazy." Pick sniffed and went on furiously. "You've been drinking, man. You know that's against the rules down here. Go sleep it off." His dark face disgusted, the engineer climbed wearily on the globe.

Baxter went into seclusion behind his steel door, which was opened with acetylene torches the following morning. They learned then what the meteorologist had been bringing in his suitcase. His locker was filled to the top with empty whiskey bottles, while Baxter thrashed oblivious in his bed, mumbling about an earth-sun. He was in a coma when a staff car brought him to a nearby clinic. The doctors said that Baxter was suffering from acute alcoholic hepatitis and might not live.

Like Baxter, the others hated to fail in an enterprise so serious, and, in the ultimate sense, they had failed, both in proving or disproving the coming climate change beyond doubt, or in finding anything but a complicated, long-range and far from certain solution—in the GPPS—if doom beckoned. Harold Anderson, who esteemed success above all else, seemed almost bitter at the outcome. He would return to Princeton shortly, he said, resume his research and hope for the best. "I'm just not convinced anything will happen," he admitted at last. It almost sounded as though Anderson wanted to forget he had ever been involved in the project.

But like the others, a perfectionist, he decided to make one last run-through with ILLIAC VII. While Baxter had been drinking himself into a stupor, Anderson had occupied the conference room. The military weather probe had continued sporadically, feeding ever more data, and Anderson asked for an update. Over the clatter of the printout, ILLIAC's staccato female voice reported

INADVERTENT CLIMATE MODIFICATION ESTIMATES REMAIN UNCHANGED. TIME FACTOR REMAINS UNCHANGED. ERROR FACTOR REMAINS UNCHANGED.

"Just like it was," Anderson muttered out loud. By then Pick had told him of the computer's COMPWATCH capability, and, to leave nothing undone on his last night at the facility, he ordered a scan of the memory banks of relevant computers to see if anything new had turned up.

The machine fell silent, and Anderson sat still, contemplating the turning globe and its mysteries, electronic and real. The eastern part of the United States lay before him in darkness, with tiny lights identifying the major localities.

He waited. The expected moment stretched on. It was nearly midnight and the silent facility seemed empty. Even Pick had gone to bed with his woman for a change. About time. Anderson thought about his own wife. She'd kill him at tennis now, for he was out of practice. What *was* the computer up to? He went to the console and punched out

user: are you functioning?
FUNCTIONING. WAIT

Anderson stood tensely, staring at the console. This was something new. Never before had ILLIAC taken so long to reply. Something preoccupied the incredible brain. Finally, unable to withstand the suspense, the climatologist asked

user: identify operation
INTERROGATING NOAA COMPUTER AT CAMP SPRINGS, MARY-LAND. WAIT

The NOAA machine! That was the one they watched most closely, because if any new meteorological data appeared for which the group was not responsible, the source was likely to be the Weather Service. The NOAA machine had been quizzed the night before; it had nothing to convey then. Suddenly ILLIAC said

ATTENTION: REVISED ESTIMATES COMING

Anderson said sharply into the mike, "Get Dr. Pick in here."

Keys began to click steadily, and when Pick, in a white terry-cloth robe and slippers, ran in, Anderson had part of the story. "ILLIAC's linked up with the Weather Service computer at Camp Springs. Know anybody named Blake?"

"I told you about him. He's the young fellow that brought the CO_2 rise to my attention in the first place."

"Well, he's running a study over there, using new data obtained on the weathership *Oceanographer* that's operating in the hot quadrant. He fed instructions to his computer today.

163

He'll learn the results tomorrow. ILLIAC's convinced something has changed. It's analyzing . . ."

"Get Finley," Pick said to the mike. As they waited he asked, "How were the *Oceanographer* data reported?"

"By radio. It's a new high-speed transmission system. The stuff goes directly to the NOAA machine."

"You mean Blake hasn't seen the figures yet?"

"Right."

"When did the stuff come in?"

"Today."

Finley entered, sleep lines scoring his face, which looked pale. "What's up?" he asked quickly.

"We don't know exactly, but it seems to be something," Pick said.

PRELIMINARY ANALYSIS OF NEW CO_2 FIGURES FROM TROPICAL QUADRANT INDICATES PREVIOUS OCEANOGRAPHER DATA MISLEADING. CO_2 RISE NOW QUESTIONABLE. WAIT

Finley's hands disappeared beneath the lapels of his robe while Anderson gulped. Pick's normally deep voice rose sharply. "Could it be . . . all that effort . . . wrong information . . . oh, Jesus . . . is it possible? I just can't accept . . . What does it mean by preliminary?"

At the console Anderson typed

user: is OCEANOGRAPHER study complete?
STUDY INCOMPLETE. MORE DATA EXPECTED TOMORROW

Anderson said, "That's that. There's nothing to do but wait."

They would have to wait until the following evening, when the NOAA facility was shut down again: the danger that ILLIAC's intervention might be discovered during the day was too great. Meanwhile, a frantic review of the project's vast

164

research commenced. It seemed, however, unshakable, unless the original CO_2 information had been wrong.

"Don't feel bad, darling," Rita said the next night, in the conference room. "The error, if there is one, isn't your fault. And an amazing job has been done here, of great value, I'm sure. Try to remember that." She laughed quietly. "Don't forget your priorities. It would be wonderful if the coming heat turned out to be nonexistent. We'll drink champagne on that."

"Right. But poor Bert, poor Murray. I feel responsible. Suppose I drove them so hard for nothing?"

"Couldn't be helped. How will Edmunston react?"

"Guess."

"We'll find you a new job—in California."

"I could do with a change."

Finley sat quietly at the conference table and Pick called, pointing to an ice bucket Rita had found. "Hey, Frank, shall we open the champagne? It's against the rules but so what?"

Finley's easy voice seemed at odds with his pallor. "To hell with the hole, huh? Yes, I could sure use a . . ."

A peremptory clacking came from the console. Anderson, stationed there, cried, "Okay, here we go."

UPDATE COMING.

"Come on, come on," Pick muttered, twisting his head in the silence.

"It won't be long," said Anderson.

"I'd like to go home," Finley murmured softly. "I'm so tired."

"Maybe it'll be all over in a couple of minutes," Pick told him. "Maybe we can all go home." The champagne bottle remained unopened. "We've had . . ."

ILLIAC reported

UPDATE. COMPLETE DATA IN FROM WEATHERSHIP OCEAN-OGRAPHER IN QUADRANT. REPORT FOLLOWS: TRANSMISSION ERROR YESTERDAY. HEAVILY CHARGED IONIC PARTICLES RESPONSIBLE. FINAL FIGURES ANALYZED. TRANSMISSION ERROR FACTOR ELIMINATED. CO_2 RISE LARGER THAN PRE-VIOUSLY ESTIMATED. REPEAT: LARGER. ESTIMATED CLIMATE CHANGE POSSIBILITY REVISED FROM 25 PC TO 50 PC. IF CLIMATE CHANGE HAS BEGUN, HEAT RISE MAY COMMENCE IN 4 MONTHS. REPEAT: 4 MONTHS. REPEAT . . .

15
CHAPTER

THE FOLLOWING DAY—Thursday—Pick stalked into Edmunston's office carrying a report that had taken him all night to prepare. As he sat down at the gleaming expanse of desk the Director said, a little warily, "Morning, Larry. Nice day, isn't it? Sun's out. Birds are singing. Taste of spring."

"Guess so."

"Hmmmmm. You feeling all right?"

"I'm exhausted and I'm feeling like you've been avoiding me, Rufus."

"Avoiding? Hardly say that. I've been busy as hell, though sometimes I wonder what doing. Can't see the forest for the details. Anyway, you've been keeping pretty scarce yourself. Got something going out there?"

The old man's expression was guarded, as it had been when he neglected to tell the Deputy that the Soviets had reported the earthquake. Edmunston knew something, Pick felt sure. "Better press the button, Rufus," he replied. Edmunston did. "About the climate thing . . ."

Edmunston turned frosty. "The question is under debate, I told you."

"That was almost two months ago."

"Something important as this takes time. There are a great

many factors to consider," the old man said, somewhat querulously.

"Time's run out." The engineer took the report from his lap and waved it. "We've restudied the matter intensively. We've . . ."

"We've?"

"I reassembled the original group, you might as well know."

"What?" The old man's anger was not quite convincing.

"You heard me. The group . . ." He paused, deciding not to tell the Director about Kline and Baxter. It occurred to him that he was worried about Finley too—the man's face had been the color of cardboard when he'd left for Florida early that morning, his work completed. ". . . has concluded that the odds favoring the change have increased fairly dramatically. The heating could start soon, as early as this summer, even."

Edmunston blinked, then turned vacant eyes toward a bar of sunlight that sharpened the colors of the Oriental rug. It was, the engineer admitted to himself, hard to accept the idea of a climate sickness on such a day. A corner of his mind heard the Director say abruptly, "Didn't I tell you to lay off this thing?"

"Listen, Rufus . . ."

"Is your group completely in agreement with you?" Edmunston asked studiedly.

"Well, I guess Anderson's still skeptical," Pick admitted.

"Anybody else know about the problem?"

"Not that I'm aware of. The Weather Service computer has new information, but we were able to reprogram it last night, using ILLIAC, so that on its readout this morning it reported the status quo. The trick worked. On a pretense I checked with Blake—you remember, the junior climatologist—before coming in to talk with you. Nobody at the Weather Service, including Blake, is aware of what's going on."

168

"Good! We can forget about this business for a while."

"Rufus, I don't understand you. This is a highly dangerous situation. I wanted to check it out carefully before making it public, to avoid a panic, but we can't wait any more. I want to get the Academy, ICSU and others involved. I need help."

"Got it all in writing, have you?" The old man angled his head toward the report.

"Yes," Pick said. "The documentation is thorough. In the conclusion I discuss the need for a period of strict national austerity . . ."

"I'd like to analyze it first," Edmunston interrupted. "Then we'll talk."

That evening Edmunston sat in Banner's office, armed with a glass of whiskey. He said, "You read what I sent?"

"I've been looking at it all day. I lost my appetite for dinner."

"Same here."

"What do you think, Rufus?"

Edmunston fondled a lock of long white hair. "Well, it looks worse than it did."

"This summer?"

"Oh, no, I don't buy that at all. Depending on what you give it, you can make a computer reinforce your original biases, and we know Pick's, toward calamity. Anyway, I'm not saying the climate change will happen at all. I only mean the odds seem poorer against it."

"And better in favor. Well, where does that leave us? It seems to me that our objective remains unchanged—to keep the President in office."

"And save the country needless turmoil if my resident pessimist is wrong. I hate sounding like a couple of conspirators, though. I'm worried that the President will look for scapegoats if this blows, and, by golly, that'll be us."

"No need for scapegoats if we can keep the lid on long enough," Banner responded.

Edmunston said, "The main consideration is Pick himself. He could be accused of revealing state secrets if he went public with it, but I don't believe he will—not easily. I know him. He's not only a loyal character but he's security-conscious to the nth. He's held several extremely sensitive positions in the government. He's got security in his bones. He drafted some of the toughest parts of the National Scientific Emergency Act. For him, blabbing would go against the grain."

"Yes, but the man has considerable influence, even a following, inside the government. He could get to the President on his own."

Edmunston said suddenly, "The solution is to get rid of the fellow. On the outside, he'd be castrated."

"I hadn't thought of that. What about the others in the group?"

The Director replied, "Well, they're liable for security too. But let's look at them. There were five to begin with, outside of Pick. Two are completely out of commission for a long time. So's a third. He just went into a Florida hospital with a massive coronary—I checked. None of them will be talking to anyone for a while. That leaves a climatologist named Harold Anderson, at Princeton. It might be a good idea to neutralize him, just in case. How about offering him a major job, maybe Pick's? He'll be under control that way. The man's deeply ambitious, and I think he'd go for it."

"You said five," said Banner.

"There's a woman. She's Pick's ladyfriend, therefore a biased witness. Also, she's a sociologist and hardly a climate expert. Still, it might be a good idea to see what we can dig up on her, in case the clearance people overlooked something."

"Why?"

"Well, to destroy her credibility, if anything does leak out. There's always a chance, and you want to control things as much as possible. The same applies to Pick. We have to be prepared to make him look bad too. It shouldn't be so hard to portray Larry as an overanxious guy who crossed the line, which is probably the truth. Most climate experts will dispute him anyway."

"Well thought out, Rufus," the Science Adviser complimented. "I think that settles things, for a while anyway."

The Director said wearily, "Yes. I'll take care of it."

It was raining again on February 25, when Pick was peremptorily summoned to Edmunston's office. As he marched down the hall, the engineer reflected that in government bad news always seemed to arrive on Friday afternoon.

The Director pressed the security button and examined his Deputy intently. "Larry," he asked without preliminaries, "could you be persuaded to forget about climate for a spell?"

"*Forget?* Jesus, here we go again."

"The White House doesn't accept the likelihood of a climate change. The White House wants to table the matter, until after the convention at least, or even the election."

"Table? That's insane. We'll be losing invaluable time. Corrective measures ought to start at once! How did politics get into it?"

"Politics is everything, Larry. Don't be naive."

"Are you trying to be funny? The general elections are a half year away. Six months could be critical," Pick said angrily.

"Don't provoke me. I'm fully aware of your concern, but

171

there are others, especially in view of the tentative nature of your findings."

"Tentative!"

"Will you agree?"

The big man said sullenly, "No, they're not."

"I think they are. Larry, I warned you in the friendliest fashion that heads might roll," Edmunston replied after a pause. "You disobeyed my orders when you recommenced research on the problem. You were asking for trouble. Insubordination can't be tolerated in work as sensitive as ours. Larry, I want you to resign."

Pick, incredulous, sat back. "What?"

"Oh, you can stay on the payroll for a while," Edmunston said, trying but failing to sound casual. "I'll work out a cover story for you, like you're on special assignment. Would you agree to accept one, in Africa or somewhere?"

"Rufus, what the hell is going on?"

"I believe I made myself clear."

"Not to me." He banged the desk top.

"That's enough," Edmunston said sharply. "I'm about to turn off the electronic screen. Every word you say on this matter from now on makes you subject to prosecution. You are to stay away from the office and under no circumstances are you permitted to visit Fort Davis, which will be shut down in any case. You're out. Understand?"

"Fuck you, Rufus," Pick said with hatred.

Gwen was nowhere to be seen. Instead, Nash, the security man, waited in Pick's office.

"Wet enough for you, Dr. Pick?" the hook-nosed guard twanged.

"Get lost."

172

But Nash didn't move. Pick was permitted to take only personal effects, few as they were. When the engineer departed, Nash even inspected his briefcase.

16
CHAPTER

When a man has been accustomed to power and prestige, he is likely to feel emasculated when deprived of them, even if the loss is beyond his control. Lawrence Pick, irrationally, experienced something akin to guilt, as if he had perpetrated a wrong and therefore deserved his plight—a sensation that deepened when he too learned that Frank Finley had suffered a major heart attack and was on the critical list at a Florida hospital.

In his Chevy Chase house, Pick was like a dissident in exile, seeing no one except Rita, taking few calls, though hating the isolation, idleness, impotence. His moods were as variable as the March weather, which vacillated wildly between various extremes. One moment he was crotchety and irascible, the next contemplative, sitting for long periods, draped in thought. On a pad before him he would draw strange configurations—circles, parabolas, rectangles, triangles, octagons, wavy lines, stars—inexplicable to anyone but him. With a grumble of frustration he would drop the pad on the floor and vanish for long periods, wearing his sweatsuit, down the back roads.

"Are you trying to qualify for a marathon?" Rita asked him one night at dinner. She had been reluctant to press him too hard, realizing how low he was. "How long do you expect to go on like this?"

"I don't know," he said with a pout, glancing distastefully at his uneaten food. "Listen, Rita, I'm difficult to be with. If you want to leave, I'll understand, and no hard feelings."

"No hard feelings! Do you want me to leave? Am I in the way?"

"No, I don't want you to leave."

"All right, but you'll have to listen to me then. Why are you just sitting around? I don't understand why you can't reach somebody in the government."

"The person to reach in the government is me, and I'm here," he said with a wry face. "There's no one else that I'm aware of who would understand the subtleties of this and have the power to act."

"The news people then. They'd have to take you seriously."

"Why? They'd soon learn I was fired, though Edmunston hasn't announced it yet for some reason. The news boys could make everything I say sound like sour grapes. And Edmunston would deny the story and find scientists to corroborate his version so you'd get nothing but confusion. I need a better way." He sighed heavily. "Also, there's the question of violating security."

He'd told her of the National Scientific Emergency Act, but not in any detail. Ironically, in terms of his plight, the Act had been drafted to give the government tools to cope with ecological exigencies like the one in question. It gave the President the right to declare a disaster emergency, and to accrue special powers without having to wait for Congress to approve his actions. A commentator had called it "an environmental Gulf of Tonkin resolution," comparing it to powers given to President Johnson to act against the North Vietnamese without having to consult elected representatives. Because, in an environmental crisis, it might be necessary to take steps without public knowledge, security provisions were harsh, and still un-

175

der challenge in the courts. But, surprisingly, many parts of the legislation were little understood. "Technically, I could be subject to arrest for leaking classified information."

"That law is practically fascism!" Rita exclaimed. She peered at him. "Still, I have the feeling there's more to it. Would they *really* try to arrest you? My hunch is that you yourself don't want to violate security because you'd be ashamed of yourself if you did. They've brainwashed you."

"Well, I did—I guess I still do—have the highest clearance. There's an obligation that goes with that," he said uncomfortably.

"You're like a priest bound to his vows. There must be *something* you can do!"

"Listen, I'd act if I could figure out how. But there's nobody to turn to, even to use as a front." He slapped the table with something like joy. "Yes, there is! What a fool I am! Of course! Blake!"

The junior climatologist appeared flattered to be consulted, delighted to have his forebodings confirmed (despite their implications), eager to put Dr. P–P–Polchak in his place after suffering so many rebuffs at his boss's hands. He was so pleased that he forgot to inquire precisely how Lawrence Pick had acquired his updated information. (Pick, for his part, thoughtlessly neglected to mention that he was no longer the Deputy Director of CRISES.)

At a corner table in a suburban restaurant the engineer, careful to reveal only what he had to, said that a new computer study confirmed the existence of a CO_2 buildup in the tropical Atlantic, and predicted that a heat rise would occur, preceded by perturbations in the world's weather, just as Blake had originally theorized. But Pick's power was more limited than Blake might think—the young man looked surprised. Pick had

176

run into a bureaucratic wall—Blake was sympathetic. Pick wanted the story out through a channel other than himself. Blake leaned forward expectantly. Blake needn't be attributed, but at least the news would come from an NOAA informant. There would be no risk to Blake's career—indeed, the world would be grateful later on. The engineer knew the name of a science reporter on the Washington *Post* who would be interested in the facts.

Like Watergate, the climate story started small—a two-inch item without a byline on a back page—reflecting the lowly status of its source. It stated that, according to an NOAA official, excess carbon dioxide in the atmosphere might bring a rise in global heat far sooner than experts had even anticipated. A period of meteorological instability could come first, and might have already started.

Probably because the weather had been so uncertain as to attract attention, the item was picked up on local TV news that day. The paper's editors, detecting interest, gave the story greater play the following morning. There was nothing new, except that NOAA denied the whole thing. But the source, still unidentified, repeated his or her assertions.

It was NOAA's Dr. James Polchak who catapulted the story into prominence. Reached at home by the science reporter, he admitted that two CO_2 studies had been undertaken in the tropical Atlantic in recent months. These tests had been routine, but Polchak, confused and naive about the press, tried to account for why he had mentioned them at all by asserting that "some dispute" existed within his department on the CO_2 issue, which was true only if young Blake could be considered important enough to figure in a dispute. Polchak tried to backpedal, but it was too late. The story reached the front page, lower left-hand corner.

By then, the Air Resources Lab at NOAA, suddenly the focus of unaccustomed attention, was astir. Under interrogation, Blake revealed that he was responsible for the story. Even so, he might have remained publicly unidentified if Polchak himself, still trying to ridicule the idea of a climate sickness when the science reporter called again, hadn't singled out a Ph.D.-less junior climatologist as the source of the nonsense.

As a result, Benjamin Blake was reached at home by the reporter. Nervously citing his original concern, he said it had been strengthened by information from another source. What source? "From . . . someone important at CRISES," Blake stammered.

When Rufus Edmunston denied knowing anything about the situation, the persistent reporter phoned Lawrence Pick, reaching Gwen, his secretary, who seemed confused. Her impression was that Pick had left the organization, though no announcement had been made. Not long after, the telephone rang in the modest house in Chevy Chase. The engineer had been expecting the call.

Yes, he was Lawrence Pick. Had he quit or been fired? No comment. Did he know about the CO_2 debate? He'd been following it. Was a climate change impending? No comment. If Pick wouldn't confirm that anything was meteorologically amiss, would he deny it? No, he wouldn't. He preferred to say nothing.

This was a case where numerous "no's" added up to "yes." On March 23, the newspaper reported that government officials were indeed worried by the prospect of increased global heat, and suggested that Lawrence Pick had been discharged because of disagreement over the issue.

Reporters telephoned, and even came to the door of the house, but, though Rita urged him, Pick refused to talk, afraid of complicating decisions which he believed the President

178

would be forced to make at this point. Again the engineer was wrong.

Almost at once, Rufus Edmunston announced the appointment of a new Deputy Director, a leading climatologist who had been a member of the research team headed by Pick that had investigated the CO_2 question in the first place. Harold Anderson was quoted as saying that the CO_2 problem had been "blown out of proportion." The quantity of the gas in the air had increased but not to critical levels. Pick, he said, was "far too pessimistic."

"The ambitious bastard!" the engineer cried from the newspaper. "He said he likes to win."

The article hinted that Lawrence Pick was unstable—a theme that was to be repeated in ever stronger form, almost as if the news outlets, the gossip mills and the general public were conspiring to make the problem disappear by crucifying Lawrence Pick. As soon as the engineer had been branded a "weather weirdo" and a "climate kook" the public began to lose interest in the CO_2 question.

Not so the more extreme elements in society. Doomsday cults announced the impending end of the world at God's hands. UFO fanciers claimed that Pick was right, but for the wrong reason—the earth's climate was really under attack from space; political fanatics declared that Russia was waging weather war on the U.S. or accused Pick of undermining confidence in the country's future. The letters, phone calls, tourists and sign-carriers outside the house made normal existence impossible. One morning, the delivery boy found the previous day's paper lying untouched on Pick's porch.

PART V
HEAT

17
CHAPTER

THERE ARE TIMES when even courageous and dedicated men lose confidence in their ability to shape events, and thus in themselves. This was such a period for Lawrence Pick, who, having sounded an alarm to which few listened, had almost ceased to care what happened to himself.

Rita took charge. She chose Huntsboro for several reasons. She had become dissatisfied with her earlier research there, wondering if she might have overlooked some small but important clue as to what might induce people to accept the reality of a coming catastrophe. Pick, she thought, might not be recognized, at least not at once, for his picture, mostly older photographs at that, had been used only sparingly, and Huntsboro, like many American towns, almost prided itself on its insulation from the outside world. Pick might find a short period of peace in which to work, and, for her, that was the most important consideration. Wanting him to resume his efforts to counteract the climate change, she was determined to prod her despondent mate into activity.

Rita compelled him to think again about the projections which he had committed to memory, since the documentation obtained in the hole remained at CRISES. Reduced to a portable calculator, slide rule and instinct, he rarefied the figures further, concluding that a period of exceptionally unstable weather would begin almost at once. If so, Rita, might get new insights about the town's response.

But spring was beautiful in Huntsboro, as in most of the country, with light rains in the dawn hours, balmy days, starlit nights. The weather was perfect for people and plants; it was especially welcome after the meteorological tribulations fall and winter had inflicted. These, though, were soon forgotten.

"Could your calculations be wrong?" she asked him uncertainly after days of almost uninterrupted sunshine.

"I don't believe so," he said. But he went often to the thermometer on the back porch. During the day it read in the low seventies and ten degrees cooler at night.

They had rented a roomy two-story house with a front lawn, comfortable furniture and a big back yard in the Dellwood section. One day Pick declared that he had a project and needed a place to work. She helped him push back furniture in an unused bedroom, where he began to construct an object out of balsa wood and cardboard. He didn't explain what it was, and Rita didn't ask, fearful of somehow deterring him.

She pretended to have settled in Huntsboro to write her book on disaster response, a story the townspeople seemed flattered by. She moved easily among them, talking, observing. George Bancroft's house lay on the next street over, so that his yard backed against hers. On a Saturday, a few weeks after the couple had arrived in town, Rita, strolling pensively across the grass, saw the Mayor's pink face regarding her across the fence.

"Morning," he said politely.

"Oh, hi, Mr. Mayor," the woman returned. "Nice day, isn't it?"

"Sure is. I don't remember a spring like this. I hope it goes on forever."

"Me too," Rita replied, smile dying. "I don't guess it will."

"No, it never does, but I'm enjoying it while it lasts. I've been working in my garden." He held up a gloved hand.

"Do you plant flowers or vegetables?" she asked.

"Both. Some stuff's up already. Want to see?"

She came to the fence. Bancroft's garden was quite extensive. About half was devoted to flowers and half to vegetables, he said. He had planted tomatoes, cucumbers, radishes, several kinds of lettuce, cabbage, corn, peppers, parsley, squash. All were above the ground. There were rows of perennial flowers too, some already in bloom. "Told you we had green thumbs in Huntsboro," he said proudly.

"The flowers are very pretty."

"You and your husband aren't gardeners, I take it."

They had decided to pose as married, hoping to minimize talk about them. "No. I hardly know one plant from another. He doesn't either, I think."

"We don't see much of that fellow." Bancroft removed his gloves. "I meant to ask you, what does your husband do for a living?"

"He's an inventor," Rita told him.

"Never met an inventor. What does he invent?"

"Oh, engineering things. He has patents."

"I've got a few ideas for inventions. I'd like to talk to him sometime."

"He's awfully hard to talk to. He broods a lot," she said, telling the truth.

"Hmmmmm. It seems like I've seen him before. You don't forget a face like that," the mayor said.

"It's quite a face," Rita agreed.

Late that afternoon, a wind began to blow over the empty tract across the street that had once been Wildwood Homes,

185

and the temperature dipped, hour by hour, until by midnight, when Pick looked last at the thermometer, it had reached 40— a decline of 30 degrees in eight hours caused by a cold front sweeping in from Canada.

In the early morning the wind shifted and the temperature rose rapidly until by noon it was as warm as the day before. Over the back fence Rita had another talk with Bancroft.

"Good afternoon, George. It's another nice day."

"Sure is. I worried last night, though. Just a few degrees colder and I'd have lost some flowers. That's the problem with spring. Things grow quick and then you get a frost and they freeze. Plants don't like the weather blowing hot and cold. Neither do I."

The pattern was repeated, with temperature dropping fast that night and rising just as rapidly in the morning. Rita spoke with Bancroft after he came home from work. The pink-faced man sounded upset. "I checked with the weatherman. It's going to get colder tonight. Pray for my plants."

Had she said prayers, they would have gone unanswered, for the night was colder and so was the day succeeding it. Bancroft walked dejectedly around his back yard. "Look at the peonies! Ruined. Some of the tomato plants too. Thank God the lettuce is OK. Have I told you I've won prizes for my salad greens?"

"What's the prediction for tomorrow?" she asked, shivering in the northerly wind.

"Just a little warmer," Bancroft said.

Warmer it was, but not a little. On Wednesday afternoon, when Huntsboro's businesses were closed, the thermometer read 80 degrees. Bancroft's face was pinker than usual. "At *last* it's really spring. I'll put in the rest of my tomato plants now," he said.

"Couldn't it get cold again? Aren't you taking a risk?"

"Unlikely. We sometimes have cool days in May, but once it turns this warm it's for good." His face turned cloudy. "But the weather's been screwy as hell. You're right. Maybe I should wait."

Fortunately he waited. The next few days were a meteorological roller coaster, with the mercury spurting up and down. It was as if the sky were a battleground of two great armies from the north and the south, struggling for victory on the unending plain of the sky. But the sun proved supreme, and spring triumphed.

"That's that," Bancroft exclaimed on Saturday. "I can do all my planting now."

But Sunday it clouded over and there was heavy rain followed by hail. Hailstones large as robin's eggs littered the mud of Bancroft's garden, breaking young shoots, knocking down plants, beheading young flowers. "Boy!" Bancroft howled with exasperation, his mild brown eyes looking up angrily. "Won't it ever end? What's the matter with the weather?"

Almost every day seemed to bring another change—heat, cold, fog, rain, strong winds that blew away the fertilizer Bancroft had just placed in a garden further damaged by each meteorological vicissitude. But it was the gardener, not the garden, that interested Rita Havu. She watched from the kitchen or bedroom window as he paced, examining the sky with a worried expression, pacing through the shambles of his green universe, bending to clip brown leaves or to uproot a dead plant, replanting, replacing, refertilizing, in a constant effort to keep order and life in his neat rows. Always, however, disorder and death prevailed, forcing Bancroft to plant again. Sometimes, thinking no one watched, he would suddenly turn his pink visage to the heavens and shake his fist.

Rita emerged in her back yard, as though by accident, and came to the fence. "Funny weather, isn't it, George?"

"Not funny ha-ha, that's for sure. I've never seen anything like it. I hate this weather—this way one day, that way the next. It throws me off. Everybody else, too. Our town just isn't the same—why, people are jumpy and irritable. Two grown men got into a fight in front of my office, a fist fight! Who ever heard of that around here? My wife has been feeling strange, too. She says it's change of life but I think it's the weather. You can't function normally when you don't know *what* to expect. Did you see that electrical storm last night?"

"It woke us."

"Us too. What a demonstration! Some lightning! It was— like the sky was being broken into pieces for a picture puzzle!" He stopped speaking momentarily and turned his head toward the garden before he said, "What's happening?"

She knew what he meant. In the morning papers, because of the unpredictable weather all across the country, speculation about a climate change had revived. The White House, the Weather Service and CRISES, through its Deputy Director, Harold Anderson, all denied vigorously that anything untoward was happening, offering proof that such unsettled weather conditions were far from unprecedented.

"The meteorologists claim that the bad weather will end soon," Rita said from the newspaper as she sat with Pick over coffee at the kitchen table. "Will it?"

"I think so," he said, staring off into space. "But only for a while. Then strange, maybe violent weather will come again. It'll continue that way until the heat starts to rise. That's how my prognosis has it."

She turned to an inside page and her face became white. "There's a picture of you!" He leaned over and inspected it. "It's not a very good likeness," she said. She read on. "Oh, my

188

God. They say you're in a mental institution somewhere, like poor Bert Kline!"

"Well, maybe I should be in one," he muttered.

"Cut it out. Will you sit there and take it?"

He said defensively, "What can I do? If the weather doesn't make them see the light, how can I?"

"Little old you," she mocked. "Well, you'll be recognized here soon. I'm surprised it hasn't happened already. Bancroft wants to talk to you about inventions, for instance. I can't hold him off forever. What does it matter if they find out where you are?"

"We'll leave," he said, as if not having heard her last sentence.

"For where?"

"New York? It's easy to get lost there."

"Get lost? Are you a fugitive?"

"Well, no," he said softly. "I . . . don't like notoriety."

"You're really something. I thought I fell in love with a fighter, not a weakling who sits on his butt all day building a toy," she taunted him.

"Toy! If you think that's a toy . . ." He controlled himself. "All right. It's related to the heat crisis. Don't ask me what it is until I know if it will work—I'm superstitious that way, and you'd only laugh."

"What do you plan to do with it?"

"I don't know. Maybe someday . . ."

She examined him carefully. "Larry, they might listen. Just might. I've been watching the people here carefully. I might be wrong, but I think I've seen something."

His sharp black eyes filled with interest. "Go on."

"Well, I stand by the conclusion of my original study—that Americans are too locked into consumption rituals to modify their habits greatly. It would take a police state to make them cut back drastically on energy use, and I have doubts whether even a dictatorship could force them. As I said, they might prefer to perish rather than change. But when I did my research I didn't take one factor into account. I couldn't, because it's not the sort of thing you're normally supposed to." She looked through the opened window at Bancroft in his back yard. "The recent weather—it's thrown these people off. I don't mean the weather conditions themselves—they can put up with those. It's the rapid *change* that gets them down." She paused as though to formulate her thoughts. "This shifting around between hot and cold, rain and sunshine. Gorgeous days interrupted by hailstones or something. A clear night and then tremendous lightning. The sudden switches bewilder, confuse, disorient them. They hate what's happening. Watch Bancroft moving his lips, talking to himself. I think he's experiencing a mild form of nervous breakdown. I imagine the whole town is."

"That's saying a lot. Anyway, what's the relevance?"

"Simply this. If an appeal like the one we've talked about is to be made to the American people, it should be during a time of great uncertainty, because that's when they're able to break out of their patterns."

"And when the weather turns normal again?"

"They'll forget about what's happened. No, the time to reach them is when they're demoralized."

They sat in silence, as he pondered what she had said, while she continued the article. Suddenly Rita cried out and slapped her hand to the paper.

"What is it?" he said.

"Nothing." She rose from her chair but sank back into it.

"Come on. Show me," he demanded.

She said in a sad voice, "Well, you'll read it anyway. It's in the last paragraph. It's about me." She hesitated a long time.

190

"Tell me."

"I don't want to because it says I was once arrested for prostitution."

He stared at her. "Rita, is it true?"

Rita slumped forward, pushing the mass of blond hair behind her ears. "True enough to serve the purpose, which is to shut you up for good. I didn't dream . . . It was so long ago."

"You'd better explain," he said stiffly.

The sigh seemed to emanate from her toes. "All right. I told you I was a sort of actress and model, right? That I gave it up to go to college? That I got by on scholarships?"

"That's what you said."

"Well, I also got money from home." She hesitated. "You wouldn't make much of a detective, Dr. Pick. You never asked me how Mother lived."

"She was an unsuccessful actress, I thought."

"You don't eat that way. And Mother never had a regular job. She worked strange hours. I never understood until I got older. In college, the scholarship money wasn't enough, and there she was, willing to help. I took the money, what she could give me."

"What's wrong with that?"

"Only that I felt I had a debt. My mother was a beautiful woman. She was still young then. She was arrested in a house they'd been watching. It looked like a jail term. But I convinced them she had nothing to do with it. I lied and said that she'd come to get me."

"What?"

"Yes. I was arrested and booked. Since I had no record I was let off with a warning. It didn't even make the papers."

"You took the rap for your mother?" he said incredulously.

"That's right."

191

"But why did she let you do it?"

"Not much character, I guess."

There was another long moment before she said, "I must know if you believe me."

"Of course I believe you. What a rotten deal."

"Thank you," she said.

"They must want to discredit me pretty bad to dig up stuff like that. Edmunston, and probably Joe Banner, must be behind it."

"What will you do about it?"

"Fight. I'm ready. Let's start right here."

Rita greeted George Bancroft over the back fence. "Hello there. You look busy."

The mayor, pulling weeds on his hands and knees, cried, "Make hay while the sun shines!"

"Yes, it's nice. Especially after what went before."

"What went before?" he asked.

"Why, the funny weather," she said.

"Oh, that. Well, you get spells of that. It'll be a great summer, according to the Farmer's Almanac."

"You buy that, George?"

"It's as good as any other prediction. I don't believe in any of them, if you want the truth." He eyed her strangely. "Certainly not in what your boyfriend says."

"So you know."

"I read a story. It had a photograph. He's divorced. And you . . ."

"I'm not important. He is."

"He's something of a nut, isn't he?"

"I wish he were," she sighed. "But he's not."

"You can't prove it by me." He turned his head to the weeds.

"How do I strike you, Mr. Mayor?"

Bancroft looked up again. "Beautifully."

"I don't mean that."

"As a very sensible young woman," he confessed. "What was said about you surprised me."

"The story about me isn't true. I wouldn't get tied up with a candidate for the looney bin, either."

"I don't guess you would."

"I tell you he's right, George. Something dreadful will happen."

"I don't believe it, Rita. I just don't. I can't."

She persisted. "Remember how you felt when the weather changed every day? Suppose it started doing that again, but even faster? How would you feel about that?"

"I told you I hated unpredictable weather."

"And unpredictability in general, right?"

"I admit it. I guess I want to look ahead with confidence, like most of us do."

"But nature has altered *its* plan. George, could you get some people together? Maybe in your office? OK?"

Burton Dickson, Andy Braden, the disk jockey, Rick Stewart, who owned the drugstore, and his wife, nurse Tuffy Beccero, Tinker Wheeler, the farmer, Cheryl Conner and her husband, Frank and Jessie Kuhn, thirteen-year-old Pinky Fleet with his parents, Betty Harris, and others—all crowded into Bancroft's office that evening to listen to the engineer who stood before them, stiff and a little shy. In the past twenty-four hours the weather had changed continually. It had been in the high 80's but northerly winds brought the temperature down to the low 60's in a matter of hours. Under clouds, it had dropped still further, but after the rain the mercury went back to the

80's again, where it was now. They sweated in the confines of the small room.

"I want to make a general observation," Pick said first. "I was brought up on a farm, as I bet some of you were." Tinker Wheeler nodded. "I remember the weather as something you could rely on. Oh, I know, it turned around—you had long growing seasons or short ones, too much rain or not enough, but in the main the weather was relatively constant. People didn't set their clocks by the weather, but they sure planned their lives on the basis of stable meteorological conditions, season after season."

He shifted from one foot to the other. "I think the weather's been changing in the last few years. Until recently, the change has been subtle, so we haven't been completely aware of it, and there's also the question of how we get information on the weather in the first place. Today, instead of simply experiencing things ourselves, we hear the reports on TV and radio, where weather is treated as news. Since news is different all the time, we assume it must be the same with the weather, and that alters our perception. To many of us, unstable weather has come to seem natural. Well, it isn't."

Burton Dickson called suddenly, "Oh, I don't know. I remember when I was in the Army. We had some lousy weather then."

"Maybe you did," Pick responded with a shake of his head, "but probably not with the wide oscillations we've experienced recently."

"Oscill . . ." Pinky Fleet whispered.

"Sssssh," said his mother.

"Big swings," Pick replied. "Think of recent weather as awfully moody."

"Like a woman," George Bancroft said with a smile.

"So the weather's been a little screwy, so what?" Dickson asked.

Pick threw a long glance about the room. "I know it's hard to take, even for me, but this weather of ours is, well, like a warning. An opening shot. I've been doing serious meteorological research on this matter, and I'm convinced that we're in for some stormy times and after that it'll turn hot, very hot."

"Why should we accept what you say?" Cheryl Conner's husband said into the silence.

"The Pentagon would have told us," Dickson said.

"Yes, why should we believe *you?*" chorused others.

"Why? The evidence is all around you. In your gardens and fields. Look what's happened in the last twenty-four hours alone!" He stared at them, then turned a morose face toward Rita. "They won't listen," he muttered.

"I'm listening!" Pinky cried.

Tinker Wheeler said slowly, "The weather's been strange since last fall. My place has been blasted twice by hailstorms, with stones big as grapefruit. I don't remember nothing like that before."

Tuffy Beccero put in, "This weather makes people so hard to get along with. You should hear them complain at the hospital. I used to be cheerful as all get-out, but not any more. This changing around makes me nervous. It's ruining my sex life."

"Now, Tuffy," said the mayor, winking at her. "Let's keep a certain decorum for our visitors. What do you have to say, Rick?"

The druggist answered, "I can tell you that tranquilizer sales have been way, way up. I have a hard time keeping them in stock. People are definitely agitated."

"The weather's all I hear about at the barbershop," Frank Kuhn pointed out. "They talk about it all day long."

"Like they're obsessed," observed Andy Braden. "I have call-in shows at the station. I hardly get time for music any more because all they want to do is rap about the weather."

"Same at the restaurant," remarked Betty Harris.

Cheryl Conner's husband said sharply, "What's the use of griping? The weather will turn normal sooner or later, won't it?"

"It won't, I'm sorry to say. Not for long, anyway."

"We have to believe him!" Pinky Fleet cried. "He's a famous scientist!"

"Ssssh," said his mother.

"I don't want to believe him but I do," the nurse groaned. "I know people, and nobody with a face like that could lie."

"Nobody accuses him of lying," the mayor said. "It's just that he may be wrong."

"He ain't wrong. I know it in my bones," said the farmer.

"How do the rest of you feel?" Bancroft asked.

Andy Braden seemed to speak for most of them. "In our souls we're convinced. The weather's nuts and no two ways about it. You agree too, George, don't you?"

The mayor replied, "Yes. But what can we do about it?"

"You already have," Pick murmured. "You've contributed to our understanding by your responses—haven't they, Rita?"

"They certainly have," she said gravely.

"I had to learn if people would believe me," he said. "That was the important thing."

"What now?"

They were at home again. "I have to return to the hole."

"What? They could really arrest you for that, couldn't they?"

He nodded. "I have to try. It's vital to what comes next.

196

That thing I've been building is crucial. ILLIAC has the information I need—without it, I can't do the final calculations. I may have something new to offer if the idea works. It may be our only hope."

18
CHAPTER

IT WAS DARK OUTSIDE when Banner's Cadillac arrived in the underground garage, where Nash, the hook-nosed security guard, waited. "Dr. Edmunston's in his office. This way, sir," he said.

"Never seen your office before, Rufus, though I can't imagine why," the Science Adviser offered as he entered the room. "Very handsome indeed."

"Well, it's a far cry from a lab. I hope I continue to occupy it," the Director said with a scratchy chuckle. "Drink, Joseph?"

"Why not? A little Scotch, please. Neat."

"Take the load off your feet."

Banner sat down and Edmunston opened a door in the dark wood paneling, revealing a bar. "I'm having cognac myself," he said over his shoulder. "Want to change?"

"Scotch is fine. Why the secrecy? What's the fuss?"

"I didn't want to talk on the phone," Edmunston replied, returning with two glasses. He seated himself, twirling the stem. He went on in a tone that was almost too easy, "I wanted to meet here because the security's better."

"Good God, man, do you think I'm being spied on?"

"Noooo. But—well, these night meetings of ours could attract attention, and you never know when somebody in the White House might decide to use a hidden tape recorder." He lowered his eyes. "You have one—I know it."

Banner opened his wider but said nothing for a moment. Finally he spoke. "What's so good about your security, Rufus?"

"I've got a device. When I press this button below my desk—" his hand disappeared—"an electronic screen starts up. It blocks any listening device outside the building. Don't like to use it too often. There's a possibility it can make a man sterile."

"You don't have to worry about that, do you, Rufus?" Banner said quietly.

"You never know about such things," Edmunston answered, sounding offended.

"What do we have to worry about this evening that makes you expose yourself to such a hazard?"

Edmunston sat back. "Pick's been located," he said. "He's in a town called Huntsboro, Virginia. It's not too far away. He was recognized by a county Civil Defense director named Dickson who, on a hunch, called the Pentagon, which called me. We have some dealings, you know. The question is what action to take. If we found him, the press will, too."

"Why do anything? Hasn't Pick been pretty well made to look foolish?"

"This highly erratic weather is just what he was talking about. I'm afraid if he reemerges he'll get people stirred up by focusing attention on the issue."

"What about the Weather Service?"

"Once a bureaucracy takes a position it's hard for it to reverse itself. They've denied that anything's wrong so often that they've got a real investment in continuing to deny it. But then, don't you? Doesn't Anderson? Don't I?"

199

"Yes. But I didn't think things would change so fast. I'm not sure I could stand up to an interrogation from the boss, and that means Pick must not be allowed a forum. I just pray to God the weather doesn't provide one for him."

"It won't. The weather will get better, you'll see. Just the same, I'd be happier with Pick out of the way for a while."

"So would I."

"Maybe it's possible to hold him until we can investigate whether he's violated security, which might take a couple of months. By then, we'll know where we stand. I have a perfect place to keep him."

"Good," said Banner.

Rita Havu recognized the curtained minibus with Maryland license plates parked outside Mayor Bancroft's office. A man sat in the driver's seat while another, burly, with a hooked nose, entered the building. She rushed home. "What shall we do?" she cried. She described the men.

"The one with the nose is Nash. He must be asking where I live. They're not trying to hide their presence, which means they're peaceable, anyway." Pick's mouth, edges turned down, stayed closed.

Nash showed up late that afternoon, alone. It was a warm day, and his shirt was streaked with perspiration. "Hi there, Dr. Pick," his twangy voice said from the doorway. "Hot enough for you?"

"It sure is. Come on in, Nash."

"Fine." Both stood. Nash said, "Dr. Edmunston wants to talk to you—in private. Something about reinstatement, but don't ask me what. He'd like to meet you at Fort Davis and suggests I bring you there. I've got a bus."

"What about Dr. Havu?"

"Plenty of room." He added, "No need to take any gear. Edmunston says it'll take only an hour or so to outline his proposal."

Pick seemed to ponder. Nash looked vaguely surprised when the engineer replied casually, "Tell Edmunston OK. Fetch us in the morning and not too early. I sleep late now that I'm unemployed."

The minibus remained outside, near Pick's old compact. At 4 A.M. they left by the back door and walked in silence through Bancroft's yard to the street, where Rita had parked the car Pick told her to rent. "I still don't understand how you plan to get access to the computer," she said when they were on the road.

"I'm banking on luck. I'm friendly with the guards, especially one of them. He used to be in charge of the morning shift and probably still is, even though the hole's not operating, so far as I know. I'm hoping he'll let me in. If not, we'll come back tonight."

"And then?"

"The security won't be anything special. I've got a gun." He patted the attaché case sitting next to him on the seat.

"You're not serious?"

"I'm afraid I am."

They reached the secret facility a little after seven in the morning. As Pick had hoped, Haggerty, the Bostonian, was on duty. The engineer stopped across from the gate and said to Havu, "Ask him to come here. Use your best professional manner." He winked at her.

Haggerty put his head to the car window. "Dr. Pick! Long time no see."

"Hello, Haggerty. Listen, I need a favor. I want to get some of my things. Nobody's up there, right?"

"Not a soul. It's all closed down." Haggerty said slowly. "Caretaker comes round every other day. He was here yesterday."

"Let me in, will you? I won't tell anybody and neither should you or your partner."

"But, Dr. Pick, I have orders to let no one in, and especially not you," Haggerty protested.

Pick reached out and punched him lightly on the arm. "Come on, for old time's sake, fellow Bostonian. I won't steal anything, I promise. And don't worry about security—I practically built this place, remember?"

Haggerty pointed. "What about her?"

"She's been here before. She's cleared."

The guard said, "Well, OK. But I'm off at three, Dr. Pick. You've got to promise me to be out of there before then."

"Promise," said Pick.

There were no cars outside, but out of habit he parked in his own slot. There was no reason for them to change into uniforms. He took the metal rod, inserted it in the aperture, and the big metal elevator doors slammed open. The elevator carried them down with a whoosh, and they entered the hole.

It was a strange, deserted world. A maze of silent activity before, nothing moved now. The glass of the control booth stared blankly; the metal tiers were empty; the great globe stood still. In the conference room, Pick activated machinery. Then, when he spoke to the mike, the ball glowed and began to turn. Though it had no place in his present efforts, the globe made the surroundings feel natural.

"What can I do?" Rita asked as he raced to the console.

"Just be patient. This will take awhile."

He opened a thick notebook he'd brought from the car, revealing pages crammed with calculations in his own concise hand. She asked, "What's that?"

"I've been busier than you thought." Punching keys, he said affectionately, "Hello, ILLIAC. I've missed you."

WELCOME BACK, DR. PICK

announced ILLIAC's breathy, female voice.

"You told it to say that!" Rita exclaimed.

"Did I? Now, ssssh."

Keys rustled in the silence. To his questions, ILLIAC flashed answers in green letters and numbers upon a small screen. The engineer seemed oblivious to anything but his interaction with the machine, as if the two had become one.

MAY 29 WED AM 8 06 27 3 . . . 4 . . . 5 . . . the digital clock snapped out. Miniseconds, seconds, minutes, an hour, two. . . . He sat, his back to her, motionless except for quick hands that riffled the notebook and touched buttons, while she watched, admiring the forcefulness exuded by the hunched shoulders, the total concentration mustered. By the time the clock said 12:52 P.M., she'd been to the bathroom twice and he hadn't budged.

Rita spoke for the first time in almost five hours. "I'm hungry."

"The kitchen is stocked, I'm sure," he muttered.

"I'm afraid to go anywhere without you," she admitted.

"Patience, then. I'm almost home."

"I wish I were—home, that is." She laughed bitterly. "Wherever home is."

Another half hour went by. He rose and muttered, "I still don't have the answers. Jesus!"

"Won't you tell me what it is?"

"Later. I have to go on. First, the can."

A few minutes afterward he was seated as before. She watched the globe slowly spinning outside the glass wall, and let herself be pulled into it, imagining a sort of gravitational hypnotism. *Home.* People didn't ordinarily think of the earth as home. Home to them was an apartment, a house, a piece of land. To them home was refuge, security, comfort. Humanity was still in its infancy. When it got older, humanity would see the *world* as its home and take better care of it—unless things happened as Pick feared.

She realized she had stared for some moments without understanding because she so little expected what she saw. "Larry," she said in a whisper. "Men with guns."

Four of them, in gray uniforms, stood on the floor below, pistols in holsters. The hook-nosed man held a microphone. His voice roared through the facility. "All right, Pick, come out. With your ladyfriend. You're under arrest for trespassing on government property. No funny business, hear?"

"I've got to hold them off. I need a little longer. It's critical I get this right," Pick said quickly. He grabbed a microphone and shouted, "Nash! Leave the hole! I won't be responsible for the consequences if you don't!"

But, drawing his pistol, Nash advanced. The shot struck the glass wall, but not close.

ILLIAC VII and the information it possessed were far too valuable to lose to enemy agents bent on sabotage or a hysterical mob that might manage to penetrate the hole. Unlikely as such events had seemed, it was sensible to plan for them, and the computer had been programmed for self-defense.

At the console, Pick punched orders. The computer's female voice said rapidly, "I HAVE BEEN INSTRUCTED THAT I AM

UNDER ATTACK. I HAVE BEEN INSTRUCTED THAT I AM UNDER ATTACK. THIS IS A WARNING. CLEAR THE FLOOR AT ONCE. I ORDER YOU TO CLEAR THE FLOOR. YOU HAVE ONE MINUTE." The same instructions were given in Russian, Chinese, Arabic and Spanish, "COUNTING. ONE . . . TWO . . . THREE . . ."

"Good God! But what's it got to fight with?" Rita shouted. "Watch!"

". . . TWENTY . . . TWENTY-ONE . . ."

He yelled, "Nash, your lives may be in danger. Get back, I tell you." But the men moved forward toward the spiral staircase that led to the conference-room level.

". . . TWENTY-NINE . . . THIRTY . . ."

Amid the maze of cabinets that were the computer's brains and body, activity began. An antenna sprouted and unfurled like the spokes of a coverless umbrella. Pick said quickly, "A heat sensor. It can detect the location of any human being in the chamber. It serves as ILLIAC's eyes." Doors opened and an object emerged.

"FIFTY-NINE . . . SIXTY. COUNTERMEASURES COMMENCING. COUNTERMEASURES COMMENCING."

The object rushed down an aisle to where the four men stood, motionless and watchful. A squat box on four wheels, its appearance explained nothing. One side of the box dropped open, revealing a metal cylinder that pointed at the human cluster. Nash raised his gun and fired repeatedly, the shots reverberating in the cavernous room. The box rolled nearer. The men ran, reaching the confines of ILLIAC itself and racing down the long aisles separating the cabinets. Suddenly the box spun, started in the opposite direction, rounded the end of a line of cabinets and met a security guard coming the other way. From the cylinder burst a small white cloud. The guard gasped, sank on his knees and retched. The machine retreated.

His companions approached slowly, and, when the box made

no attempt to menace them, seized and dragged the guard to the open elevator. Steel doors banged shut.

Rita cried, "What was that stuff?"

"Something like Mace. The effect is only temporary. ILLIAC could have killed the man with gas if it wanted to."

"DEFENSE SUCCESSFUL. ATTACK HAS CEASED," ILLIAC chanted. "ALERT CONTINUES."

"Will they come back?" she cried.

"I don't know."

"Can't you shut down the elevator?"

"It wouldn't matter. There's a stairway they can use."

"How do we get out?"

"We can't right now. But we can hole up practically forever. They can disconnect the telephone but not the radio, so we can send messages." He paused and added, "Nash is a stubborn son of a bitch. He's been ordered to get me and I think he'll try."

"How did they learn you're here?"

"Who knows? They must have showed up here looking for me, and Haggerty had to tell them. It doesn't matter. Why don't you get something to eat? I have to finish."

"Eat? I won't leave you. How can you work at a time like this?"

"No choice."

A half hour later the elevator opened without warning. The computer announced, "DANGER. CLEAR THE FLOOR. DANGER. CLEAR THE FLOOR. DANGER. CLEAR THE FLOOR. DANGER. CLEAR THE . . ."

The four men moved forward, slowly, eyes on the squat metal box that waited before ILLIAC. The umbrella-like sensor quivered delicately. Nash had straps over his shoulders and one hand behind his back; the others carried rifles, and one guard raised the gun to his shoulder and fired. The machine

206

flew backward on its little wheels, crashing into a cabinet, then started toward the guards again. A bullet, ricocheting off the box, ripped into the computer.

"DAMAGE," ILLIAC reported in a matter-of-fact voice.

"Oh, my God," the woman said.

"Not serious," Pick said from the console.

The four spread out as the box on wheels approached, flap down, the gleaming metal cylinder twisting. As the muzzle fixed on Nash he brought out the hidden hand. In it was a nozzle. He pressed, and a jet of flame spurted across the chamber, touching the mobile box with fiery spume. The smoking box crashed into a metal cabinet.

"DAMAGE," ILLIAC diagnosed unemotionally. "COMMENCING FURTHER COUNTERMEASURES."

Pick bent forward, touched keys and watched numbers flash on the screen in a green torrent. "Nash," he thundered into the mike. "You've hurt the computer. Nobody's going to thank you for that. I urge you to get out of here." The engineer returned to Havu's side. "He won't listen, the idiot."

Again the gray uniforms advanced toward the spiral staircase. The two in the conference room could see what the security guards could not. In the four corners of the cavelike chamber rods on swivels turned rapidly. Beads of light appeared in them. The first guard up the stairway staggered, clutched the railing and fell back, bouncing down iron rungs to the floor. There was no blood, merely a brown hole in the center of his chest.

Nash screamed, "You'll pay for that, Pick!"

The computer, deliberately, it seemed, withheld its fire, as if testing the intentions of the trio, because the rods followed them across the room without lighting up. The guards ran toward the elevators but at the last moment they veered and took refuge in the aisles of ILLIAC.

207

There was no outward sign of movement. Pick seized the mike and shouted, "It's a standoff, Nash. Leave. I'll guarantee your safety." In answer, a guard emerged from the computer banks and ran in a low crouch toward an overhanging metal tier, reaching cover. With a quick motion he turned, raised the rifle to his shoulder and fired. Near them glass shattered and a small hole appeared.

"Get back! He's aiming at us!" Pick switched off the lights and the conference room was dark except for the pale-green glow from the computer screen. The two came forward again, invisible from the outer chamber. Peering up, the rifleman left the metal overhang, as if to get a better view, appearing to forget the lethal tubes attached to the ceiling. The antennae quivered, and a rod swung and lit as the guard turned his face. He dropped on his back. The body possessed one eye.

Rita put a hand to her mouth.

Nash and his companion remained hidden inside ILLIAC's perimeter, with the laser guns pointed in their direction. But the weapons didn't fire even when Nash chose to show his head for an instant above the line of cabinets.

"Why?" she asked.

"ILLIAC's afraid of hitting itself. You'd be too, if you cost fifty million bucks," he said coldly.

Outside, the deadly pantomime proceeded in total silence. Nash continued to poke his head above the boxes or out to the side of them, with the laser guns shifting as they followed his movements. Then, from the opposite end of the file of cabinets, the other guard appeared, rifle stock to his cheek, aiming for the swivels that supported the rods. He was an expert marksman; a laser gun fell to the floor, followed by another. The rifle pointed at a third, but beams came together like the blades of invisible scissors. The guard's head sagged, as if attached to his neck only by a loose string.

Nash's hand crept from the bank of computer cabinets and seized the dead man's rifle.

"*Why* won't he give up?" Pick raged. He called into the mike, "Nash, what's the matter with you? Why won't you get out of here?"

"Fuck you, Dr. Pick," Nash said. His words, carried through the open microphones in the chamber, sounded oddly hollow and faint, as though the sound system had begun to fail.

ILLIAC reported with new urgency, "I AM UNDER ATTACK. DAMAGE. LOSING CORE."

"What's core?"

"Information. Capacity. I don't understand why." A billow of smoke rose from the computer compound. He yelled, "Oh, shit! Nash is using the flamethrower on it. He's burning out its guts!"

The two remaining laser rods slumped in their swivels, muzzles pointing down dejectedly. "LOSING CORE," ILLIAC said, speaking more quickly, voice higher.

"I'm going out there! He'll destroy my machine!"

"He'll destroy you. That's what he wants! He's crazy."

"My gun." He reached for his case.

"Larry, for God's sake, stay here!"

"I can't. Wait for me." He ran to the console, pressing buttons feverishly. "Come on, baby, try. Do your best. Just one final run, OK? You've enough stuff left. I need you. *I've got to have those numbers.*"

"PRINT-ING," ILLIAC said weakly.

The engineer, out in the chamber, could smell oily smoke with the pungency of burning wire. He had bought the revolver in Washington when the crank calls started, more worried about Rita than himself, but he'd never used the .32 and barely knew where the safety catch was. The gun felt puny in

209

his big hand. Why hadn't he procured a more powerful weapon? As quietly as 210 pounds on size 14 shoes permitted, Pick crept down the metal stairway to the floor of the hole, gun ready. Above, the globe turned slower than normally. Spark-filled smoke rose from ILLIAC. If one reached the globe's flammable plastic carapace . . .

ILLIAC's insistent voice sounded in the chamber. "I AM HURT. MY CIRCUITRY IS DAMAGED. I AM CONFUSED, REPEAT, CONFUSED. I NEED MORE CORE. GIVE ME MORE CORE."

Pick reached the maze of cabinets behind which Nash was hidden, and pulled himself up on them. Peering over the edge, he could see some of the ravages wrought by the flamethrower —burned-out metal panels, melted glass, dripping insulation. Smoke poured from ILLIAC's charred brain segments. The security guard must be revenging himself on the machine for the death of his comrades; he was out of his senses or he would have gone topside for help.

Nash was not in the aisle. He could be in the next one over, or the one after that, in the checkerboard of computer cabinets. Pick lowered himself to the floor and clambered on top of the next bank. As he prepared to poke his head over, gun in hand, he heard the hiss of fire, and acrid smoke billowed in his face. The engineer tried to stifle a cough but failed.

"GIVE ME MORE CORE," ILLIAC demanded.

Nash's voice said, surprisingly genial, "Come on down, Dr. Pick. I know where you are. Just take it nice and easy. If you've got a gun, drop it to the floor."

The engineer flattened himself to the surface and examined his surroundings. It occurred to him to crawl to the end of the bank, leap up to the Lucite maintenance rungs of the globe and be carried away, out of Nash's sight, but the ball's revolutions had ceased. Not far from him, in the other direction, was the stem of ILLIAC's umbrella-like heat detector, its long spokes extending out over the cabinets. He wondered how much weight the contraption would bear. . . .

"Come down!"

Pick said nothing, and Nash loosed a jet of flame that shot past him, close enough to sear his hands. A wisp of smoke appeared on the face of the motionless ball.

"The globe's on fire!"

"I don't give a shit. Come down!"

"All right," Pick shouted, pushing the pistol over the edge and hearing it clatter on the floor. Pick rose to a crouch, like a sprinter, muscles straining, and leaped, his body arching over the aisle, painfully catching a thin spoke, grateful for its tensile strength. Below, Nash, turning in surprise, struggled to raise the heavy flamethrower. Pick, carried by the metal wand, flew over him and dropped, smashing the guard in the chest with his feet.

"MORE CORE," said the smoldering computer. "DANGER."

Nash reeled backward into a cabinet while Pick went to his knees. Before the engineer could rise, the guard had slipped the canister of chemicals from his back and was up, advancing. He was big, almost as big as Pick; his mouth was menacing beneath the hooked nose. He knew his stuff, Pick could tell from the extended fingers, stiff like clubs. Pick waited, still on his knees, shaking his head dazedly. Then, with one fluid motion, the engineer pushed hard, body straight, ramming past Nash's hands, crashing into his chest with the blunt instrument of his head. Nash gasped, fell backward, rose and ran. Grabbing the pistol, Pick chased him.

Nash rounded the end of a computer bank and started down the aisle. Before Pick could stop him he had clambered onto the cabinets and stood, momentarily uncertain, as Pick climbed. Nash leaped, catching a Lucite maintenance rung and crawling to the surface of the globe.

"I AM LOSING CONTROL," ILLIAC declared.

Nash climbed higher, evidently planning to jump to one of the tiers and escape up the stairway. Pick raised the pistol but lowered it. Killing wasn't his line. Nash went up quickly. But the guard was no longer moving of his own volition. The globe had begun to turn again, trailing smoke from a smoldering patch that expanded rapidly.

As he reached the tier, Nash started to jump from the ball but it lurched and spun faster. The guard, nearly striking his head on the overhanging metal lip, dropped flat on the globe's surface, securing himself to the rungs with his hands and feet, hanging helplessly. Faster and faster the globe whirled, until the surface of the ersatz earth became blurred. The black patch spread out, obliterating oceans and continents. Fanned by the rushing air, flames sprang so that the globe resembled a giant pinwheel.

Pick had no means to aid Nash; face down, feet squeezed into a maintenance rung, the guard rode supinely on the earth's whirling back as the fire approached. The computer screamed hysterically, "I AM CONFUSED, REPEAT, I AM CONFUSED. MY CIRCUITRY IS BADLY DAMAGED. I DO NOT UNDERSTAND WHAT IS HAPPENING. I AM LOSING TOUCH WITH REALITY. IN THE EVENT OF A SUCCESSFUL ENEMY ATTACK, I AM TO SELF-DESTRUCT."

Pick raced up the stairway, attempting not to breathe in the smoke-filled chamber, to the conference room, where Rita screamed, "What do we do now?"

The engineer, ignoring her, stepped to the console and issued commands. "ILLIAC's berserk. I can't contact it." He turned to the printout and stared in surprise. The paper was filled with complicated equations. "Jesus," he shouted, "ILLIAC did it! She did it! Good girl!" He typed hastily and green words appeared on the screen.

Pick grabbed the printout and threw it with the pistol into his case. He cried, "Come on, Rita, let's go."

"I AM TO BEGIN THE SHUTDOWN PROCEDURE. COUNT IS SIXTY SECONDS. COUNTING . . . ONE . . . TWO . . . THREE . . ."

"There isn't time to reach the elevator," Pick shouted. "The stairs."

They moved out on the narrow catwalk attached to the walls of the chamber and ran. Close by, the globe whirled, creaking on its axis, showering flame and debris as it began to disintegrate. Again and again the prostrate form of Nash rushed by, face expressionless, eyes open and unblinking as a sheet of fire covered him.

"Hurry!"

"I can't run any faster."

He seized her hand. "Come on!"

Nash's eyes were closed when his burning body passed again.

The entire surface of the globe was aflame now, crackling like lightning. The rail of the catwalk was becoming too hot to touch. They pressed close to the wall, shielding their faces, coughing in the smoke.

"FIFTY-FIVE . . . FIFTY-SIX . . . FIFTY-SEVEN . . . FIFTY-EIGHT . . ."

They reached a doorway in the wall. From the top, a mesh of heavy wire descended. "Rita! Dive!"

They lay on the floor, panting, as the grate shut behind them.

"OK. Come on. Let's go."

"Rest a minute."

"Can't."

Reeling with effort, they climbed six stories up inside the hill, choking in the smoke that filled the stairwell from the

213

inferno below. When they reached the open air he still cried, "Hurry," as he prodded her to the automobile. They swerved down the twisting road to the gate. He yelled to Haggerty, "The hill's about to explode. Jump on the car." Tires screeching, he raced toward the narrow bridge without railings, almost going over the side. He stopped.

"Larry," Rita shrieked as the ground began to shudder. The top of the hill vanished with a roar and a cloud of smoke. When it ended there was a hill with a cone on top, like a volcano.

19
CHAPTER

NASH HAD USED the word "arrest." If arrest had been threatened for illegally entering the hole or whatever could be trumped up in the name of security, what might he be accused of now? The newspapers attributed the blast to an explosion at an Army ammunition dump that claimed four lives. There were no living witnesses except Rita to what had happened six stories down in the hole; if prosecution proceeded, who would accept their version of how the guards had died? Not many. Pick could be tried for murder.

He would have returned to Washington anyway, despite the risks, but he wanted to finish work on the new design for which ILLIAC had furnished its last-gasp calculations: the "earth-sun," as Baxter had called it, might well be critical to the world's future. That would take him no more than a week or two. Then he would confront Edmunston, Banner, the President. He'd go to the press. He'd carry a sign in front of the Weather Service. By whatever means, the engineer intended to deliver his message.

In early June, still incognito, Pick and Havu moved into a small sublet apartment on New York's Fifth Avenue, overlooking Central Park, with a terrace affording a clear view of the sky. The engineer scored the sociologist for expensive tastes, but the tall, impersonal building was exactly what he wanted.

As if the skies themselves conspired to hide the truth, the weather turned lovely again with bright days and moon-filled nights.

A week later, as the engineer was deep in his designs, strange weather began all over the country. In New York, a tornado and a hurricane visited back to back.

The towering tornado touched down near Passaic, New Jersey, causing severe damage, devastated Hackensack, crossed the Hudson River and crashed into the docks, tearing off piers and sinking small craft. Leaping the West Side Highway, the black funnel then marched into the city itself, gaining speed as it whirled down a side street, breaking windows, tearing down awnings and signs, overturning cars as it proceeded to Greenwich Village, where it caught hundreds of sightseers gathered to watch its passage, ignorant of the power involved, by surprise; dozens died trying to flee.

In Washington Square Park, the funnel, overarched by deep-gray clouds, paused, swaying like a gigantic dervish, became viviparous, giving birth to another tornado, quickly equal in size and wind velocity to the original. The two twisters, as though part of an orchestrated effort, separated and went south on different avenues, followed by a procession of police cars, fire trucks and ambulances, flashers flickering, sirens screaming. One of the odder incidents of that already strange afternoon occurred when a twister stopped, leaned backward, and seemed about to retrace its journey. No motion picture could have duplicated the farrago of twisted metal when the lead vehicles tried to turn around.

But the tornadoes stayed on tracks laid by lines of buildings on either side of them, passing through Little Italy, Chinatown, the municipal area containing City Hall (even then pre-

216

occupied with another budgetary crisis the storms would soon augment), and Wall Street, where the air was filled with paper, sucked through broken windows of stock exchange traders. At last the two funnels joined in Battery Park, where, after returning a new landfill to the harbor, they wandered over the bay, creating for a finish a spectacular waterspout.

"DOUBLE WHAMMY," headlined the New York *Daily News*, but, as Pick noted, no connection was made between the severe disturbances and a larger, far more portentous climatological event.

Few seemed to grasp the hurricane connection, either.

Hurricane Abby, the first one of the year, having wracked Florida, boomed north, keeping at sea until she shifted suddenly and headed straight at New York City. So rapid had been her pace that tropical birds that had taken refuge in the storm's eye and couldn't get out of it were still alive when the hurricane crossed the city, where the birds managed to escape. Groggy from the tornadoes of the day before, New York failed to react promptly to the fast-moving storm, which, the prognosticators had said, would strike elsewhere; most people, in any case, refused to believe that a major disaster could follow another. The winds, whirling at 150 mph, with a terrible, low-pitched shriek, found highways still clogged with motorists. Hundreds of cars were overturned. A 14-foot tide inundated the coast and forced the evacuation of thousands, then exposed to heavy winds and prodigious rainfall. These people were lucky compared to those trapped on low-lying islands connected by bridge or ferry to the mainland. Fire Island, crowded with summer residents, was almost completely covered by the raging sea; the bay was awash with the wreckage of houses. With 12,000 dead, it was the worst tragedy ever to occur in the United States.

The exceptional tide put the lower part of Manhattan underwater. Escaping gas and short-circuited electrical lines caused explosions and fires with which the fire department was help-less to deal. At mid-afternoon, when the eye reached it, Times Square was almost dark. On streets strewn with broken glass, twisted metal, bricks from facades, fallen marquees, and human bodies, ambulances crawled carefully. The scene was duplicated in many parts of town.

The city made a surprisingly fast recovery. It was as Rita Havu said: in a post-disaster period, people helped each other. Maintenance personnel worked round the clock to re-store essential services. Thousands answered the calls for vol-unteers: cadres toiled in buildings, streets and parks to clear the wreckage. Even schoolchildren aided in rescue and care for the wounded. The racial divisions of the city were forgotten as black and Hispanic volunteers labored in white neighborhoods, and whites in theirs. There was little looting despite the ab-sence of security, and crime in general virtually disappeared. As a television station observed editorially, "This has been our city's finest hour. Although it took a devastating hurricane to prove it, New Yorkers are capable of brotherhood, sacrifice and unity. Let us hope good will come from this tragedy."

But by and large the city continued to ignore the factor that would alter its destiny.

Early Friday evening Pick returned from a university computer, where he had been running his last tests. He found Rita on the terrace pouring charcoal into a small outdoor grill and bent to kiss her, murmuring, "Your skin's so cool."

"Feel the breeze. Delicious, isn't it?"

He watched the trees gently tossing in Central Park, ten stories below. "Let's enjoy it while it lasts. I heard a report today from a ship at sea." He had bought a shortwave radio and listened frequently. "It's hot out there. If the wind changes . . ."

218

"Stop worrying for a minute. Make us a drink. I'll have gin and tonic."

"Eating outside?"

"Don't you think so? I'll throw a couple of steaks on. We can watch the sunset."

"How wifely you sound. Have I tamed the shrew?"

"Yes, dear."

On his way to the bar he flicked on the television and stood for a moment before the six o'clock news. The TV face was saying, "The bulk of the scientific community takes the position that there is no relationship between the recent unsettled weather and a climate change. They see a temporary disequilibrium that could bring us some bad storms this summer. For more on that here's . . ."

"Larry!"

"Hang on a minute, Rita. I'm watching the news."

"Come here at once!" she ordered shrilly.

His frame filled the open doorway. "What is it?"

"Feel the breeze."

"We went through that already," he complained. "It's shifted, that's all."

"No. It's different. There's something in it now."

"Do you *smell* something?" he asked, perplexed.

"*Feel* something. In eddies. Bits of . . . It's gone. No, there it is again. Little fingers of . . . heat! Yes, heat!"

He stepped to the railing, palm upraised. "Honey, your imagination is working overtime, unless you have a fever you didn't have a couple of minutes ago."

"Stand there a minute."

He probed the air with all his senses. "I don't . . . yes, I do. Hot fingers, just like you said. Could there be a fire nearby?"

"There's no smoke."

"I want to hear the forecast." He returned to the TV, drumming his fingers on the top of the set as he watched a commercial for suntan lotion. Unable to wait, he took the phone and dialed the weather forecast number. "Good evening. These are the 6 P.M. readings from the National Weather Service. Temperature, 87 degrees. Humidity, 65 percent. Barometer, 29.6. THI 70. Fair skies predicted for tomorrow, with warmer weather, perhaps reaching 90 degrees. Chance of rain, 30 percent. Winds from the southeast . . ."

He heard the report through twice before returning to the terrace with another impatient glance at the TV set. "Hot day predicted for tomorrow. It's supposed to hit ninety."

"It's nearly ninety now," she said, peering at the thermometer that hung on a wall. "It's gone up in the last few minutes."

They stared into the twilight, drinks and steaks forgotten. The incoming breeze was filled with a complex and changing pattern of temperatures, strands of cool air mingling with warm. Rapidly the dusk was heating up.

"What's the reading now?" he asked her, some time later. Rita lit a cigarette and read the thermometer by the match.

"Over ninety."

All around them they could hear the roar of air-conditioners. Figures emerged on adjacent terraces to stand mutely. "Rita, I wonder if . . ."

"You think . . . ?"

"Yes," he said, "it's here."

He went inside, picked up the telephone, dialed *The New York Times* and asked for a science reporter he had met at conferences. "Dwyer? This is Lawrence Pick."

"Pick! Where are you calling from?"

"New York."

"Oh. Are you . . . all right?"

"Sure. Why?"

"I thought you were in a . . ." Dwyer's voice trailed off.

"Listen, Dwyer, do you have an updated forecast on tomorrow's weather?"

"Strange you should ask. I was just looking at it. It's going to be goddam hot tomorrow."

"How hot?" he asked tensely.

"They're talking about over a hundred. It's supposed to go up fast."

"It's going up fast now."

"It is? It's air-conditioned here, of course. Think this climate change you've talked about could be related?"

Pick said, "Yes. I think it's starting."

"What? Are you sure?"

"I'm almost sure."

"May I quote you?"

"I hope to God you do," he said heavily.

At once, Pick went to work at the telephone. A guard at CRISES said the Director wasn't there. No answer at Edmunston's home, either. He raised the Executive Office Building and learned that Banner was out of town. An attempt to reach the President of the United States was of course fruitless, but he left his name and number.

A few moments later the phone rang. "Dr. Lawrence Pick?"

"The same."

The male voice identified itself as belonging to a Presidential aide. It was neither friendly nor hostile. It said, "Wait."

"Wait? How long?"

"I don't know. You'll be contacted."

A hot breath filled the night.

The heat wave that began suddenly on the evening of July 1 struck the eastern seaboard like a physical presence. In New York, as in many other places, it was well over 90 degrees by 8

221

A.M. of July 2. By noon, the mercury stood at 101—a record for that date—reaching 102 by late afternoon. Gradually it sank back to 95 and stayed there throughout the night.

Heat was a cumulative discomfort; on the first day, while people sweltered, they took the caldron in stride. Millions, seeking relief, fled to parks and beaches. It was also a day for sharks, brought closer to shore perhaps by the exceptional warmth of the Atlantic water. Dozens were sighted in the morning. The beaches were closed until the afternoon. Police in helicopters shot many and no more were seen.

On Friday evening, July 1, the President of the United States had gone to Camp David, as he did every long summer weekend. This one, though, was to be different, and there had been warnings.

A U.S. Senator from Virginia had been under intense pressure from a growing group of constituents centered about the town of Huntsboro. They drove him crazy with letters, phone calls and delegations. Convinced that the climate offered a serious hazard to the future, they wanted governmental action and the reinstatement of one Dr. Lawrence Pick. The Senator did not take the citizens seriously, but, to discharge his obligations, he mentioned the matter to the President at a White House breakfast.

The President personally did not read a great deal of his mail, but there were two letters an aide thought he should see. One, occasionally unintelligible, and characterized by many crossed-out sentences, underlines and exclamation marks, was from a hospital in Denver, Colorado. The other came from a hospital in Washington, D.C. Kline and Baxter made the same point: that the danger of climate change was real. Then a long intelligent telegram arrived from Florida which the President also read, having asked to be given any communications pertaining to meteorology.

222

Neither the President nor his inner circle were any better equipped to understand the complicated problem before them than the ordinary citizen. Nonetheless, as a politician, he had keen instincts, and, as President, he took his responsibilities seriously. For him, the climate question had existed only as one more of the dreadful but implausible scenarios conjured up by scientists—but no longer.

When the heat suddenly immersed the East Coast, the President summoned Joseph Banner to Camp David. He asked the Science Adviser bluntly if anything was wrong with the weather. Banner tried to equivocate, but the President persevered. At last the Adviser revealed the division between Pick on the one hand and Edmunston, Anderson and himself on the other. There was still no proof that Pick's assertions were true, Banner claimed, and in any case the group believed that there was enough time to nominate and reelect the President first and worry about the climate later, if such was necessary.

On Saturday the President ordered Rufus Edmunston in. The heat was increasing, and both the Director and the Science Adviser were nervous. Again the President reviewed the facts, seeming to withhold judgment, but he called the National Security Council into session. Neither Banner nor Edmunston was asked to attend.

On July 3, in New York, with forecasters promising that cool air would bring relief, the temperatures went higher. It was 100 at 8 A.M., 102 by noon and 103 by mid-afternoon. A mass exodus commenced, with flights to cooler places completely booked. The Automobile Club of New York reported "extremely heavy traffic" and "unforgettable" traffic jams. The mood of the city was torpid, with a few tourists wandering desultorily down empty avenues. Department stores, open on Sunday, attracted crowds, however, as did all places with air-conditioning. Power supplies were nearly normal and the heat wave was not yet intolerable because of the low humidity. Besides, the public believed it would end quickly.

Although Pick's warning made headlines, the news media continued to concentrate on irrelevant statistics and human-interest stories: the jogger who quit halfway round a reservoir because his glasses steamed up and a metal chain around his neck gave him a burn; the woman who provided free lemonade on the street. There were 25,000 cars at Jones Beach. A typical report said, "Some people ambled through green preserves, like Prospect Park, or went ice skating at indoor rinks, where the temperature was a comfortable 60 degrees. In one, Bernard Glickman was practicing for an exhibition he planned for his wife and friends for his forthcoming birthday party. Mr. Glickman will be eighty-five years old." Bernard Glickman died the following day from heat prostration.

On Monday, the fourth of July, greater difficulties started. Several degrees cooler than the city, the beaches and country-side offered a small dispensation from discomfort, but the problem of getting there began to make the effort questionable. Key bridges, raised for small boats, refused to close because the metal in them had expanded, and traffic was backed up for miles until repair crews lowered them. Buckling pavement closed sections of major highways, and where they were open the large numbers of stalled cars made progress torturous. In the city, softening asphalt forced the police to barricade various streets, and overheated cars blocked tunnels and bridges.

To make matters worse, air pollution began to rise, adding to fears about public health. The death rate jumped, especially for the elderly. "People already debilitated don't do well in heat," explained the Chief Medical Examiner, adding that the toll would be far greater without air-conditioning, which, for the old, provided a life-support system. Would the power fail as it had before in New York's history? A spokesman for Consolidated Edison, the utility, insisted that aside from regrettable neighborhood blackouts there was no danger of a widespread breakdown. Was it true?

One well-publicized event seemed trivial, but not for long. It started when a handful of people undressed in Central Park and were arrested for nudity. Incarceration in a non-air-conditioned jail was cruel, unusual and even lethal punishment, but hundreds, sensing the rigid absurdity of the law, defied the ban on public nudity and took off their clothes. The exhausted police abdicated. Their lack of energy, widely perceived, led to a sharp increase in robberies and contributed to the riots of the following day.

Heat dominated the city's life—massive heat, descending in sunlight, lying in pools on the sticky streets, rising in dense eddies, crawling up the sides of tall buildings, reaching a sky that was unnaturally yellow by day and tinged with green at twilight—few cared why. Throughout much of the United States the same heat prevailed, and was explained by the Weather Service as being the result of three high-pressure areas forming a nationwide "heat conspiracy." "They work," said a meteorologist, "as companions. The spacing between them is such as to make optimum conditions for unnaturally hot weather. There is little cloud cover, so the land is deprived of shade and rain. As the air sinks, it reaches higher pressures near the ground, and the compression makes the air still warmer. The unfortunate truth is that the hotter it is the hotter it gets."

On Monday the temperature hit 105 at 10 A.M. The only records mentioned now were the high of 106, set on July 9, 1936, and of 107 on another July 4, in 1966, at La Guardia airport, where the sun beat down on wide stretches of aprons. On this day, however, it reached 109 there, despite the stupendous odds against three days of 100-plus temperature. With the death rate hanging like a pall over the city, the heat proved more than the human body and spirit could bear.

". . . the death rate today was almost eight times normal. Dr. Irene Wise, First Deputy Commissioner of the Department of Health, has this advice: 'People over sixty-five should go out as little as possible. Lie around and take it easy. All others should avoid physical exertion, like running after trains and buses, as much as possible. Don't eat heavy meals; increase your consumption of liquids, with the exception of alcoholic beverages, which have a dehydrating effect. Use heavier dosages of salt with foods, unless you have a cardiac condition.' 'Dr. Wise, would you tell us how effectively the human body can acclimate to heat?' 'Studies have shown that men, when suddenly exposed to a very hot environment—say, 120 degrees Fahrenheit and 20 percent relative humidity, or, 91 degrees and 95 percent humidity—were unable to work effectively and exhibited a wide range of symptoms, including fatigue, lassitude, dehydration, hypertension, depression, suicidal tendencies. But in four to ten days they adjusted somewhat.' 'Do you see any signs of New Yorkers adjusting?' 'Frankly, no. But the study I mentioned was done on young men in perfect physical shape, which a great many of us are not in.' "

Rita put down a small bag of groceries, turned off the radio and called, "Are you alive?" When there was no answer, she went to the open bathroom door and looked in. "Larry, are you sick?"

Pick lay cramped in a bathtub full of cold water, eyes closed. "I'm OK," he muttered.

"Poor baby! This heat drives you nuts, doesn't it? But you can't stay there all day. It isn't good for the skin. Larry, you've got a rash on your leg!"

"Heat rash." He struggled from the tub.

She went to the bedroom and changed into a bathing suit and then they went out on the terrace, he in a cotton robe. She fanned herself with the evening paper whose headline read, "HOW LONG CAN IT LAST?"

"You're perspiring already. Wouldn't you be cooler inside?"

"No. Either the air-conditioner isn't working right or the power supply is down." He inspected her. "You're hardly sweating, Rita. It isn't normal."

"The heat doesn't seem to bother me as much as other people." She put her head over the railing. "Look at the crowd in the park! How would you like to have to sleep there? Even if the power fails, we have the terrace. Count your blessings."

"We're lucky, all right," he said. "At least we can jump."

"Don't talk that way even as a joke. You're becoming morbid." She blinked at him. "Did they call when I was out?"

"No," he said sullenly. "I've tried Edmunston and Banner, too—again and again—but I can't find them. I don't know how long I can . . ." He paused and went on quickly, "I'll be better when the heat breaks. It has to, soon."

She smiled weakly. "Promise? It's been three days since we made love, and that's a record, too."

"It's too hot for fireworks," he complained.

The traditional Independence Day celebrations were canceled.

Tuesday, the fifth, began deceptively. Early-morning showers brought the temperature down to 90 degrees, which felt almost comfortable by comparison to what had gone before. Heavy rain followed by cool air was promised by the Weather Service once again. Believing the worst over, citizens went about their customary lives.

By 9:30, however, with the city functioning more or less

normally, the mercury started up once more, under a sun so bright it was hazardous not to wear sunglasses outside. The thermometer read 100 by 11 A.M., 105 by one, 107 by 2 P.M. and, at four, reached 110 degrees. It was 112 in Atlanta, 113 in New Orleans, 115 in Chicago, 116 in Houston and 120 in Los Angeles. Such temperatures could have been tolerated in a dry climate, but the humidity had been increasing rapidly, too, in New York, and stood at 60 percent—typical of the country.

The Weather Service could not be blamed for being wrong—the atmospheric conditions were beyond its experience—but, just the same, the riots of that morning could be accounted for by the frustration felt by people who, having expected the heat to end, realized they must continue to endure. One flash point was at the corner of Fifth Avenue and 100th Street, where police tried to turn off a hydrant to conserve the diminishing water supply. A mob materialized and attacked the officers. It grew in size until it became a small army that looted and pillaged, contrary to Havu's earlier assumptions.

In the business districts the situation was not much better. It was evident that the only reason electricity had been adequate was that the preceding days had been a long holiday weekend. As the day got hotter, pressure on the generators grew, and as a precautionary measure air-conditioning was reduced in office buildings, which overheated rapidly. Workers were ordered home, too late. By then, in the tall towers whose windows could not be opened, plate glass had been smashed and office equipment of all kinds, large and small, rained on the streets. The buildings were eventually evacuated, but by then, movement throughout the city had become difficult.

Asphalt paving softened until roads, and even airfields, proved useless. The subways ran, though slowly, and without refrigeration to save electricity. Of the thousands of emotional crackups that occurred that day, many happened on crowded subway cars where body heat and lack of ventilation raised the temperature still further. Commuter railroads operated irregularly, since it was feared that tracks might bend. Many people, instead of trying to go home, decided to wait for the restoration of normal service. They went to the air-conditioned apartments of friends, or jammed restaurants and movie houses—anywhere that was cool. When the power failed in the early afternoon, and the heat continued to rise, travel anywhere in the city became impossible.

The only benefit conferred by the scalding temperature was the end of unrest: turmoil took effort and almost any effort was too great. Literally millions of people took to the streets after the power failure drove them from air-conditioned refuge. Stuporous, gasping men and women leaned or squatted in the shade against the sides of buildings, waiting for a breeze to riffle the still, oppressive air. They stood at water fountains to wash their faces and quench their thirsts. Some limped on bare and blackened feet, having lost their shoes in the swamp of soft asphalt. Jewelry was left at home—metal of any kind became too uncomfortable to wear. Some even tore at themselves, as if their own skins conspired to make them hot.

Just as humans displayed symptoms of sudden madness, so did the animal population. Among the problems preoccupying health officials was the emergence of countless rats, driven from their lairs by the temperature; roaming freely in buildings and streets, they bit viciously. Dogs and cats, too, seemed deranged. They growled or hissed, bit or scratched at those who approached. Caged birds showed similarly aggressive tendencies, as did zoo animals, whose attendants were afraid to feed them. The worry was that the animals might cause an epidemic. This danger was compounded by the difficulty of burying humans, who died in extremely large numbers after the electricity failed, both from natural causes and suicide.

229

In that temperature, decomposition was rapid, and there was the problem of how to move the bodies, since vehicles could no longer use the gluey streets. Repulsive as it seemed, the plans were to carry corpses to makeshift graves in the parks. Crematoriums went unused.

The loss of electricity, which occurred in almost every major American city during the heat wave, was, of course, a catastrophic event, and proved once more the complete dependence of urban localities on power. It was not merely a matter of losing lights, elevators, subways, air-conditioning and so on down the litany of facilities operated by electricity. In the extraordinary heat, the question of food spoilage became critical. On the radio (many stations possessed auxiliary generators and stayed on the air for those who had battery-operated sets), citizens were warned either to eat fresh foods immediately or throw them out. For instance, at 110 degrees, an opened jar of mayonnaise became a toxic substance in a matter of hours. They were also instructed to keep garbage in their dwellings, since garbage trucks could not use the roads. This injunction was generally and understandably defied, with the result that, as evening approached, a terrible stench began to spread through the city from rotting food that lay in the streets crawling with rats.

The extreme discomfort experienced by the general population was heightened, certainly, for those incarcerated in jails and mental institutions, and the authorities confronted a dilemma between the needs and rights of those forcibly detained under now intolerable conditions and those of the public at large. In the end, a combination of riots and mass suicides within the institutions forced officials to decide to free all but the most violent cases. A new element of instability resulted. By then, planking had been placed over the asphalt quagmire, and it was possible to move on foot about the city on the concrete sidewalks, which stayed firm. Muttering, yelling, screaming people shuffled aimlessly in private worlds, oblivious to anything but the casserole in which they cooked.

By evening, crowds congregated at various spots. The fences around reservoirs had been scaled with ropes, and thousands lay in the water, itself the temperature of a tepid bath, despite warnings of drownings and contamination. The parks offered standing room only, but even that was better than the streets, which regurgitated the heat accumulated during the day. There was no respite, no escape.

In places of worship, jammed multitudes sought help from on high. Wet skins gleaming in the candlelight, bodies pressed together, huddled in subdued silence while half-clad ministers, priests and rabbis prayed for deliverance. The people prayed with them.

At 10 P.M. the temperature rose again, to 112. The inferno of night, thick with the stench of garbage, was rent by the screams of humans and, from the nearby zoo, wild animals. Even Rita Havu, who had seemed almost immune to the heat, cried out in frustration and agony as she stood on the terrace, a desolate, immobilized Pick on a deck chair at her side.

To keep him preoccupied, she told him what she saw: on Fifth Avenue sidewalks a long aimless procession with kerosene lanterns; in the park, hundreds of flickering torches and a slow-moving cortege of wagons loaded with the day's bodies for burial; as elsewhere in the city, buildings burned out of control, the raging fires illuminating the sky. . . .

The phone rang at 7 A.M. Rita picked it up, listened and shook him, handing him the receiver. "It's them."

He'd managed only a few hours' sleep. He tore himself awake and said, "Yes?"

It was the voice he had heard before. "Dr. Pick, you're

needed in Washington. Don't worry about the explosion at the . . . ah . . . ammo dump—that's a dead issue. Airports, roads and railroads are still closed. Can you go to the roof of your building at once? An Air Force helicopter is standing by."

He could already hear the thrash of blades in the distance.

20
CHAPTER

WHEN THE HELICOPTER carrying Lawrence Pick landed on the White House lawn, he was brought immediately to the President's office. The man seated between the flags looked and sounded different than he did on TV, being somehow harder, more abrupt and much colder than he permitted his smiling public image to convey. Nonetheless, strength was what was needed now, and that the President appeared to have.

The two were alone. "The situation, as I understand it," the President said in a voice of deep concern, "is that we're in for greater heat. Right?"

"Much greater, sir," the engineer replied, hoping that deference would not be required. "It will amount to a larger climate change than the world has ever experienced. Human survival cannot be taken for granted."

"That seems grim enough," the President answered. "Are you sure?"

"Yes sir. Quite sure, I'm afraid."

Silent for a moment, the President said suddenly, "I ought to resign."

"Resign?"

"Resign. Quit. Abdicate. Who wants to preside at a time like this?"

"But if you don't, who . . . ?"

"I know, I know," the man said sullenly, as though angry at what history was about to do to him. "All right, let's get started. I've determined that no existing government body is competent to handle this. A new organization is required, one with enormous powers."

"I agree."

"The obvious candidates to head up the Task Force are no longer in government service." The President's smile was not meant to be friendly. "Dr. Edmunston is out, and so is Banner, the fool. If it were worth the effort to try to put them in jail, I would."

"Harold Anderson?" Pick asked rapidly.

The President sliced his throat with his finger. "Also out. Anderson came to me to say that he'd been wrong, but in the end I don't trust his judgment either. Which leaves you to lead . . ."

"Oh, no! I wasn't destined to be a public figure," Pick lamented.

"I wasn't destined to be the last President of the United States, either, but it looks like I might be," the President sighed. "Yes, yes, I've read your report, not that I thoroughly understand it. We have to do what we have to do. Now tell me, in plain English, just what is required?"

The engineer spoke of the solar-energy satellites that must someday girdle the earth and beam power from outer space. He told of the vital need to keep thermal pollution as low as possible in the interval. He came at last to the earth-sun, though he used a technical term for it as well.

"Just what is that?"

"I brought a model of it, but they wouldn't let me take it

into this room. Security, I guess. They don't understand what it is."

The President pressed a button and spoke, and the men waited until two aides laid the contraption on the President's desk. Pick had had a glimmering earlier, but the drunken rantings of Murray Baxter had put the solution in his head. He'd built the model in Huntsboro, perfected the calculations with ILLIAC and completed the task in New York. The complex system was the first of its kind.

"You see here," Pick said calmly, forgetting completely that the man across from him was not simply another scientist, "what would be a massive arrangement of huge mirrors. They would focus the sun's rays on central receiving stations as shown here, here and here. Then—am I going too fast?"

"I follow," the President grunted.

"The function of the ground stations will be to retransmit the heat by special laser beams to an orbiting emitter, represented by this ball-like object that looks like a large balloon. It will disperse the heat into space. The emitter's necessary because . . . You want the details?"

"Definitely."

"Because the beams will not have unlimited range. By themselves they'd fail to take the heat completely out of the atmosphere, which is mandatory if we're to have a chance to succeed. The emitter will blast the heat into space. We'd put it up by rocket, of course. The specs for the rocket are . . ."

"That's OK," said the President hurriedly. "How long will it take to build this gadget of yours?"

"I figure we can get a small prototype a year from September, with luck. If it works—and that's a big question—such devices will have to be orbited all over the world until the power satellites can do the job. Otherwise it may get too hot too fast. There won't be time to test it fully on the ground.

Either it functions or it doesn't, in which case the chances for human survival are even smaller." He paused and went on, "But we can't hold up the power satellite program to find out. We don't have a year to waste."

"How do we know if the earth-sun works?" was the President's simple question.

"Instruments. Though, as a matter of fact, primitive as it sounds, you'll be able to tell just as rapidly by the naked eye, depending on cloud conditions and what time of day it starts to operate. If it's functioning, the contraption will become incandescent. It'll light up like an electric bulb."

There was no question now. "You'll accept then."

"Yes," said the engineer, "on two conditions."

The President bristled. "What?"

"That you'll put your entire prestige behind the effort, and that you'll be frank with the people."

"I'm always candid. What's there not to be candid about?"

"You'll have to tell them that we might fail."

Looking older than his years, the President stared at him. "All right," he said finally. "I will."

On national television, the President discussed the colossal effort that would be needed, introduced the man he had chosen for one of the most important jobs in the world, and cited the proposals that Congress would have to enact. One was to delay the summer nominating conventions—the Republican Convention was about to open—and the November elections until the situation was clarified, to keep partisan politics out of the picture. The President would stay in office an additional year. Congress concurred, but on other proposals it dallied. Many legislators remained dubious about the fundamental changes required, as did the people who had elected them.

Convincing Congress to accept the inevitable once and for all was the weather itself. Meteorologically, the summer was extraordinarily difficult. Due to the heat, the country was disrupted by massive hurricanes, tornadoes, droughts, floods and fogs, most of which materialized without warning, so that the weather seemed to change day by day. Uncertainty about what to expect, plus the growing danger the weather represented, finally made Congress, still in session in August, fall in behind the engineer after tumultuous debate.

As head of the new Energy Task Force on Thermal Pollution, Pick had been running about the country to recruit scientists, inspect industrial sites, and speak to large but somber crowds for whom the message was always the same: Time is in short supply and may be running out. We've got to hurry, all of us, or humanity will lack a future.

Even before the summer ended, a massive effort—financed from E for Energy Bonds, with wage and price controls to keep down inflation—was underway, involving thousands of scientists and engineers and a labor force that would ultimately number more than one million, which took up the slack in employment. At Cape Canaveral, Huntsville, San Diego, Seattle, Long Island, and dozens of other places formerly involved in either space or defense, the production of power satellites began.

Time, he emphasized. The real focus in those early months was the prototypical earth-sun. The collecting cells and the transmitting equipment were under construction around the clock, closely watched by foreign observers.

Time. Geography and industrial production would conspire to make the United States and Canada the first victims of ever worse heat. What could be done was to keep the thermal pollution as low as possible, and thus add vital years to the calendar.

Time. Throughout the country, in village squares, parks,

237

busy intersections, special clocks were placed. These clocks, in red mountings, had large white faces with a red hand and red letters that gave the months instead of hours. The months began and ended with September, when the earth-sun was scheduled to be sent into orbit. The clocks were meant as reminders to save energy because time was short.

There were two basic thrusts that critical year. One involved the construction of elaborate equipment and facilities meant to counteract the effects of global warming; the other the reeducation and indoctrination of the American people.

But the "Energy Czar," as the press termed Pick, was far too busy to oversee both operations, and it was, in fact, Rita Havu, the disaster sociologist, who supervised the campaign to limit consumerism. Working with Pick in a wing of the Executive Office Building, next to the White House, she tried first to analyze the problem for him.

"*Any* people faced with the imperative to change as fast as we are asking ours to do would find the process extremely difficult. In the case of Americans, consumerism, modern as it may seem, has really come to amount to a form of social organization, and is as much a determinant of how people live, think and believe as the class system is in Britain, or village society in Asia. There was a study that showed Americans to be the second most religious people in the world, in terms, at least, of what they *said* about themselves—India, I think, was first—but, if you ask me, household gods are the real ones. Status, comfort, success, conformity, and so on—all indices of social performance are ultimately based on the output and use of consumer goods."

"Meaning what?" he said, busy with a pile of papers.

"Listen to me. This is important. Meaning that the social upheaval required will be fully as profound as that instituted by the Communist Chinese—and they had a much longer period. It won't be merely a matter of eliminating waste and convincing people to make do with what they have. Ultimately they will need something to substitute for getting and spending, which might involve a higher level of consciousness, especially in the areas of sharing and human compassion. But, before that, the consumer habit must be broken."

"How?"

The first step—enforced actually by the Department of Commerce under special powers from Congress—was a ban on the production and use of a number of domestic items deemed nonessential that required energy and produced heat. The list included power tools and lawn equipment; appliances like electric blankets, electric toothbrushes, electric can openers; garbage-disposal units, microwave ovens, and so on. As time passed, the list became longer. Unnecessary driving was forbidden, along with all frivolous consumption of energy.

Rita Havu insisted that people think collectively. Why did everyone own cars when they lay idle so much? Why not have neighborhood automobiles, cooperatively owned and garaged, so that one could be picked up as needed? There should be more emphasis on public than on private property, more stress on sharing, more group spirit. She recommended self-entertainment, like card games or music, rather than spectator sports or color TV, both of which required outlays of energy in large amounts.

Astonishing changes occurred in subsequent months. As consumers, or ex-consumers, the public grudgingly complied, though often at the insistence of a new kind of police called Energy Wardens who wore red uniforms and were empowered to remove electrical equipment from private homes if their owners exceeded the prescribed limit of power. Heat output

239

was monitored, too, from roving trucks equipped with thermal detectors to locate violators by triangulation. Gasoline rationing was instituted and automobile trips of less than one mile prohibited except for emergencies, a provision which proved difficult to enforce. Cars with less than two passengers were forbidden to use the federal highway system, but public transportation was greatly strengthened. Vacation trips beyond a certain radius were outlawed. The public was encouraged to use bicycles, which sold for little since the government subsidized them.

Inconvenience, discomfort and some suffering resulted from the stern measures and the dislocations they caused. In reaction, dissident cults appeared, devoted to preserving the American way of life, specifically consumer goods, to which their followers prayed at private ceremonies, with the secrecy of spiritualists. In Missouri, Indiana, Ohio and western Pennsylvania, and many other places, whole sections went into armed revolt, counting on the central cities to come to their aid—which failed to happen. To a greater degree than the small towns and suburbs, the cities seemed to understand that the day of the consumer had ended, at least temporarily.

As part of the campaign to discourage their use, many consumer goods were depicted as not only unnecessary but ugly and even foolish.

Anti-commercials encouraged women and men to launder clothes by hand; to cultivate a natural look that required no hair sprays or expensive clothes; to like cheap, easy-to-make, simple furniture; to wash floors with soap and water; to travel by railroad rather than planes; to burn wood fires rather than fossil fuels; to grow their own vegetables; to . . . the message was always the same. America at its outset, when there was a frontier and a new land to conquer, was a frugal society with simple ways that ought to be imitated now.

This message, reproduced on radio, billboards, in leaflets, employed everything from ponderous warnings about the climate change to ridiculous slogans on how to have fun without causing thermal pollution. "Get Hot but Don't Make Heat— Up with Sex," said one. The panoply of advertising, public relations and publicity was devoted to the theme that a simpler existence, far from being unpleasant, was actually preferable.

There was adequate food, clothing and heat that first winter. People quickly ceased to miss, at least with any great intensity, the sociologist maintained, the so-called labor-saving devices and luxuries they had previously held indispensable. Many sorts of work, she said, could almost as easily be done by hand as by machine—and there were benefits. Pride at being able to do things for oneself increased; and older people, previously deemed useless, helpless or both, discovered they could fend for themselves and even for others.

Another important result was to propel people out of private worlds they had once considered inviolate. The very rich yielded to social pressure and became something of an anachronism. Cloistered housewives, forced to use public facilities to machine-wash clothing, were part of a community that shared. The commuters, forced into car pools, made new companions. For many, there was a sense of unified purpose. A large number of individuals, in short, learned that the machine had succeeded in making them atomized, isolated and lonely—or so the propaganda claimed.

But the overriding reason why Americans finally accepted the many changes being forced upon them—despite Havu's argument to the contrary—was because they were compelled to concur in their necessity. The fact of a climate change was becoming increasingly indisputable. Snow that winter fell only in the most northerly parts of the nation, and even there it soon melted. Rainfall was abundant, though, and in the stroke of a

241

single year winter became the growing season in many parts of the country where cold had prevailed before. The summer, Pick warned, might be too hot for agriculture, and it was vital to stockpile food and water for emergencies.

Each summer, according to the engineer, would be longer and hotter than the one before, until summer met summer in an endless season. Already that spring, tropical vegetation crept north.

In June, Pick and Havu returned to New York. The efforts they had begun were proceeding satisfactorily, and he was asked to coordinate a concerted international anti-thermal effort, headquartered at the UN. The summer was hot, sometimes brutal, as July turned into August. But this time preparation reduced suicides, crime and death by half.

21
CHAPTER

FRIDAY, SEPTEMBER 5, 1981. At four in the afternoon Pick walked in the door. Rita said, "Hello. You're early. Did the UN blow up or something?" He had been working seven days a week.

"No." Pick patted his dark face with a handkerchief as he fell into a chair. "There's too much anxiety there to get anything done. The place is shut down through Monday." Monday was Labor Day, when the earth-sun launch was scheduled.

"Have you decided whether to go to Canaveral?"

"I don't think I will. I'd only be in the way, and we'll know the results as fast here as there." He hesitated. "Anyway, I wanted to spend this weekend with you, alone."

"You make it sound like we won't have another one."

"Maybe not. There are some new figures coming out tomorrow. The heat's greater than we expected. It looks more and more like the earth-sun's the only chance we have." He shrugged. "Besides, I don't like traveling in the heat. You heard the forecast?"

"Yes. It might go way up."

"Jesus," he complained, "I can't take it. I weighed myself today. I've lost twenty pounds this summer."

"That's one loss you can afford," she said, anxious eyes

belying the jocular tone. Pick looked pale and gaunt. "Listen, why don't we get away for the weekend? To the mountains, where it's cooler anyway. Don't we deserve it after what you've been through? I've got friends in the Berkshires. You can commandeer a helicopter. Call it an inspection trip."

"We'd never make it. They're dug in there. Every access is patrolled by those trying to keep us city folks out." He laughed contemptuously. "The fools think they're safe from the heat. If a runaway greenhouse starts, even the Himalayas will turn red-hot sooner or later. Anyway, do we want special treatment?"

"I guess not," she said. A deeper shade of pink flushed her cheeks.

He yawned. "It's stifling in here. How do you stand it, Rita? That lousy fan does no good at all. Let's move to the terrace." All air-conditioners had been removed so that no one was tempted to use precious power, but small fans were permitted on exceptionally hot days.

For those fortunate enough to have one, a terrace had become a focus of life, with plastic shields that could be lowered around the sides during rainstorms, which happened frequently, tables for meals (mostly sandwiches), and mattresses on the deck. Rita and Larry slept outside, and not just at night, for siestas had become the custom. Between the terraces clotheslines were strung—Rita waved at the woman next door who was pulling in her laundry. (Elsewhere in the city clotheslines were strung across the streets, so that New York resembled a vast American rural backyard, washer-dryers having been forbidden.)

At the railing Pick squinted behind dark glasses in the glaring sunlight that filled a molten sky. The city had changed greatly. Damage from the six hurricanes that had struck since spring was extensive—fallen trees lay everywhere. Across the park, buildings that had burned during the fires remained boarded up, in the absence of energy or funds to rebuild them. Central Park was different, too. Because of the heat, the rain and the abundance of carbon dioxide in the atmosphere, sections were overgrown with thick vegetation and bright flowers, like a jungle, with swamps and streams. Thousands of tropical birds, deposited by the hurricanes or escaped from the zoo, squawked in the branches, flashing with vivid colors.

"The park would be lovely if it wasn't so ominous," she said, beside him.

"And if it didn't stink from dead fish." He slapped at a stinging insect. "Rita, let's take a walk. It'll probably be too hot tomorrow and I need the exercise. Besides, I want to get my mind off the launch."

"What's the temperature?"

He looked at the thermometer. "One hundred five."

"I'd better take a parasol."

The summer before, their costumes would have seemed unbelievable but no longer. On Fifth Avenue Rita Havu wore a bikini, while Pick was in khaki shorts and a sleeveless undershirt. Both had extra-dark glasses and special shoes with wide soles that wouldn't sink so easily into the soft asphalt.

The streets were jammed. Many people had been relocated outside the city, but there was a limit to the numbers the camps could absorb, and others preferred the city since the heat was unbearable in the country too. (With the sand too hot to walk on, the beaches stood empty.) The crowd moved slowly, in Arab caftans or burnouses, ponchos made of sheets, bathing suits, underwear, loincloths, jockstraps, or nothing—except on their feet and heads. To shield oneself from the powerful sun had become a necessity; those who didn't carry umbrellas or parasols wore sombreros, big floppy hats, conical straw hats like Asians in rice fields, or pith helmets, as Pick sported.

They joined the shuffling throng, careful to avoid the touch

245

of burning skin. "Whew!" Rita exclaimed. "Oh, for deodorants. Did *they* have to be banned too?"

"Not essential."

"Well, people smell."

"Can't be helped. Maybe we do too."

"I took three cold baths today, you rat."

"Not me."

"You don't deserve your girlfriend."

A man looked up at Larry. "Aren't you Dr. P—" he began, but lowered his head again, muttering, "It doesn't matter."

Entering the park, they passed musicians playing languidly for a slack-lipped audience. "What's that song?" he asked.

She hummed, then said, "It's a song about how it's too hot to make love."

"Jesus!" he said with distaste. "Who does *that* any more?"

"I wish we did." Her oval face turned wistful. "You remember when I told you—God, how long ago it seems—that I didn't want to get married? I've changed my mind."

"Oh?" he said dully.

"If we survive, promise that you'll marry me," she persisted.

His dry mouth laughed hoarsely. "Only a woman could be romantic when it's a hundred and five in the shade."

"One-oh-six," she corrected him. "I just heard the radio." Many carried transistor radios with which they followed the weather reports, issued endlessly, listening for the slightest indication that the heat might end.

He panted a little and said, "Oh, well."

"Promise me."

"I promise, honey, if we make it."

She peered at him. "Larry, are you frightened?"

"Scared to death. Aren't you?"

"Yes. So's everybody. Look." She pointed.

Many had come to believe in the supremacy of the devil, whose hell seemed to have arrived. Under a tree a group in loincloths huddled, the women bare-breasted. They seemed to be praying to a fat man leaping before them whose skin was covered with red dye through which ran runnels of sweat. A forked tail had been attached to his jockstrap, and on his head two horns had been placed. A clumsy set of cloven hooves was fastened to his feet, and he carried a scepter. Shrill laughter shrieked from between white teeth over a pointed beard.

"Lucifer, save us," the group moaned.

"*Ha–ha–ha–hiiiiiii.*"

"Save us, Lucifer."

They moved away and the chanting faded. This time he pointed. "Jesus, look there." A scrawny middle-aged woman lay on the grass, arms outflung, head to one side. She was dead. Flies covered her body.

"I can't," Rita said, closing her eyes.

"That's how the world ends, not with a bang or a whimper but with insanity and death," he said. "I'm not waiting around for it."

They had hinted before at a suicide pact, but now confronted it openly. She said, "What will you use? They aren't permitted to sell sleeping pills and we don't have any."

"I still have the gun."

"You'll kill me first, promise? And immediately."

"Yes. I guess I've made two promises today. I wonder which I'll have to keep."

Saturday, September 6, the temperature rose higher. By then, 110 degrees with high humidity, while hardly supportable, no longer seemed like conditions on a distant planet. This was Spaceship Earth, and what was happening in Bangor, Los

Angeles, Podunk and Xenia would happen sooner or later to Bangkok, Leningrad, Paris and Zanzibar, when the heat caught up with them. From everywhere on the globe messages of good will, sympathy and hope poured in. Even as the weather knows no frontiers, so the barriers between men and nations crumbled in those critical days and hours.

In Yuma, Arizona, on Sunday, the temperature achieved 160 degrees. In New York, the mercury reached 118.

Too weak to move, Pick had taken the phone from the hook, tired of the endless ringing. The work in Florida would proceed without him. Rita had gone out for canned food, and the engineer, in a deck chair on the terrace, sipping a warm soft drink through a straw, felt helpless, almost delirious. The flies and mosquitoes buzzing about him had been joined by insects from the tropics with terrible stings. He flailed his arms listlessly and let his mind run. It came to New York years from then if the heat rise continued. Greatly shrunken by the rising sea, the city would resemble a huge Mayan ruin, with the tall buildings covered with creepers and moss. Perhaps crocodiles would float in the lakes and reservoirs, wild animals graze on streets carpeted with grass, vultures fly overhead. Around the city would be jungle inhabited by small bands of humans gradually reverting to savagery in suffocating heat that made civilized life impossible. Maybe hunting parties would come to the island in canoes over rivers swollen by the ocean, in search of food.

What color would the survivors be? Black, he felt sure, because the pigmentation was better suited to strong sun. Black people would stay black; the other races, if there was time enough (no one really knew how long such adaptations took), would turn black, too. But they wouldn't have long, in any case. If the mounting heat didn't kill them the anoxia would. And then? Condition Venus.

The countdown at Cape Canaveral, followed by an anxious humanity via radio, began at 8 A.M., with the launch scheduled for noon. All morning a vast network of mirrors had been directed at a series of collectors, which, using briefly the entire power supply of the eastern United States, would retransmit the energy to the orbiting earth-sun. What remained problematical was whether the transmitting beams could carry the load. If the system functioned, power sources would be provided for it.

At 11 A.M., however, the countdown was stopped by mechanical difficulties. It resumed at three, halted again, started once more at 6 P.M., and recommenced shortly after nine. Pick and Havu sat on the terrace, while below them, illuminated by dim street lights, a dark crowd waited in silence.

"It won't be long now," Pick said, listening to the din from the transistor radio. "They're on the final countdown."

"We have a little while."

From the deck chair he could make out her face from the small bulb burning in the living room. The blue eyes with swollen lids managed to look eager. "Rita," he gasped. "You don't want to . . ."

She went to the living room, extinguished the light and returned to stand by him, saying coquettishly, "Now?"

"Jesus, how hot is it, honey?"

She took a flashlight from the table and shone it on the thermometer. "It's only a hundred and seven."

He said with a moan, "I can't, I just can't."

"You can!" she cried. "This might be the last time, darling."

"Rita," he protested. "There's nothing I'd rather do but . . ."

"You don't have to do anything," she breathed. "Lie back. Don't move. Easy. I'll do everything."

And she did.

"I love you."

"Love you, Havu," he said sadly.

A great cheer came from the radio. The rocket, aloft, thrust ever deeper into the stratosphere. From it gushed the next stage, rushing into the hole of space. There, long wands extended, drawing sheets of silvery metal, until a circle was formed.

If it worked, other, more powerful devices would follow. Mankind would have to survive a few terrible years, but then the heat would abate and, when the power satellites went up, the crisis would be over. The earth could become paradise, just as the Bible believed it had begun. And perhaps beginnings were endings, and endings beginnings.

Something that shone above meant salvation; a dark sky was the end.

The lights went out as the transmitters sucked power. The crowd below cheered and then became silent as every eye probed the moonless night. Darkness . . . the heat death . . . or . . . The seconds stretched on, an infinity of moments. Rita's hand touched his frowning face. "Don't lose hope," she whispered. "Keep looking up. Don't lose hope." Empty blackness. Nothing. *"Keep looking up!"*

The death of dreams, he thought bitterly. At least he'd had forty-two years and above all he'd had Rita. Be thankful. He visualized the squat pistol in the dresser drawer, beneath a sweater for which he'd have no more use. A bird screeched in the void—the only sound. His eyes seemed sightless. He lowered them to the luminous dial of his watch. Too long. It was over.

"Keep looking up!" she cried.

He went inside, opened the drawer, groped for the gun, clicked the safety catch. On the terrace again he stood behind her lean white back as she gripped the rail, head elevated. "I love you," he said. He raised the pistol.

"Larry," she murmured. "Wait. There . . . look!" she screamed. He dropped the pistol and pulled her to him.

The earth-sun flickered, died, reappeared, grew stronger. A new light, round, yellow and steady, gleamed in the heavens.